D1082051

freedom song

———

'It takes us further "towards a home in the heart"
than Chaudhuri has before. Its final, subtly elegiac section
reveals Chaudhuri's overriding concern: the slow unfolding
of personal trajectories around the dull pages of national
narrative. Succinct as a miniature, this saga draws half a
century of public and private histories into a few months'
AAMER HUSSEIN, *Independent*

'Subtle and strong . . . the narrative flits from mind to mind,
flashes forward and back, finding a great and casual beauty
at the edge of the haphazard . . . Amit Chaudhuri's subject,
in this tender and capricious book, is inexhaustible'
ADAM MARS-JONES, *Observer*

'Chaudhuri puts his finger on the Bengali pulse . . .
In this saga of Bengali life, situations and moments are
lovingly strung together . . . Chaudhuri deserves praise for
telling us that a part of that world still exists. It is a very
reassuring feeling'
Literary Review

'Amit Chaudhuri evokes the background noises of Calcutta
so effectively that even for a reader who has never set foot
on the sub-continent there is an eerily realistic effect'
PENELOPE LIVELY, *Spectator*

AMIT CHAUDHURI was born in Calcultta in 1962 and brought up in Bombay. He is a graduate of University College, London, was at Balliol College and later Creative Arts Fellow at Wolfson College, Oxford. His first book, *A Strange and Sublime Address*, won first prize in the Betty Trask Awards, the Commonwealth Writers Prize for Best First Book (Eurasia) 1992 and was shortlisted for the 1991 *Guardian* Fiction Prize. *Afternoon Raag* won the 1993 Southern Arts Literature Prize and won the Encore award for Best Second novel. His work has appeared in various publications including the *London Review of Books* and the *Times Literary Supplement, Granta* and the *New Yorker.* He is married and lives in Cambridge and Calcutta.

AMIT CHAUDHURI

freedom song

PICADOR

First published 1998 by Picador

This edition published 1999 by Picador
an imprint of Macmillan Publishers Ltd
25 Eccleston Place, London SW1W 9NF
and Basingstoke

Associated companies throughout the world

ISBN 0 330 34424 2

1 3 5 7 9 8 6 4 2

A CIP catalogue record for this book is available from
the British Library.

Typeset by SetSystems Ltd, Saffron Walden, Essex
Printed and bound in Great Britain by
Mackays of Chatham plc, Chatham, Kent

I am grateful to the Arts Council
for a Writer's Award during
the writing of this book.

IT WAS a solitary voice, saying Allah-hu-akbar and other familiar but incomprehensible syllables. Though it was coming from quite far away, for the nearest mosque was a mile northward, she could hear it clearly, as if it were being recited in this very lane, and its presence filled the grey area between her sleep and waking. The singer, if one could call him such, seemed absolutely absorbed, wherever he was, in the unearthly lift of the melody, in his indecision between repetition and progression, and in the delicate business of now prolonging and now shortening a syllable. The city was still — the trams, the trees whose leaves were covered with a film of dust, the junctions, Lower Circular and Lansdowne roads, the three-storeyed houses on Southern Avenue, the ten-storeyed buildings on Ballygunge Circular Road. Soon that machinery would start working again, not out of any sense of purpose, but like a watch that is wound daily by someone's hand. Almost without any choice in the matter, people would embark upon the minute frustrations and satisfactions of their lives. It was in this moment of postponement that the azaan was heard, neither announcing the day nor keeping it a secret.

She got up, as she had been getting up for fifty years, ever since she was fifteen years old and became serious about her singing, going out into the drawing room in the house in Shillong to practise, so as not to wake up her sleeping brothers or suffer their cheerful mockery. The morning today was almost as cold as the mornings in Shillong used to be; she was slower now, her hips wider, as those of a woman who has borne children are said to be, and, at this moment, a little unsteady on her feet. Solemnly, she put a shawl around herself and disappeared into the darkness of the bathroom, as if she had a rendezvous there, and, ten minutes later, emerged again. Her husband was asleep, his outlines barely distinguishable from the quilt. Her own quilt had become a bunched-up, higgledy-piggledy mess, and seemed to have a small child hiding underneath it.

When she came out of her room, she found the door to the guest room open. The curtains had been parted, and the single bed already made. As she was looking around, the knob on the bathroom door turned and Mini came out, her spectacles misted, patches of wet on her blouse and petticoat. She had always been a clumsy girl. The bathroom, whose window faced east, was flooded with light.

'What, Khuku!' she said with great surprise. 'You're up already?' Then, a note of both respect and affection entering her voice, she said, half to herself, 'Shib must be asleep.'

'I was woken by the azaan,' complained Khuku. 'And, believe me, Mini, I had no sleep last night, I began to think about Bablu and I lay wide awake with my head feeling hot.'

'Really!' said Mini, feeling outraged on her behalf, and seeming to speak of a group of absolutely tiresome schoolchildren (for she *was* a schoolteacher), 'They are going too far! And,' she said, 'it isn't really Indian, it sounds like Bedouins.' With a look of satisfaction on having said this, she began to comb her hair, which was wavy, not very long, and still all black. Then, hobbling towards the dressing-table, she stood opposite her reflection, exactly as dark and stocky as herself, and began to sort out, with both hands, the folds of a white sari with a green border, tucking it in first into the petticoat that had been tied not only above stomach-level, but almost approaching the chest; chin lowered, she drew the layers of the sari around herself till she was almost completely ensconced in it. 'Bas!' she said when it was done. 'Now we can go outside.' But Khuku had already slipped out silently to the hall and was telling Nando to get up.

'Get up, you lazy man!' she commanded him. 'Give us tea!'

Nando went on sleeping. She went around the hall aimlessly, like an insect exploring a window-pane, and then entered the room her son stayed in when he came back from America; the beds were perfectly made, all his books were standing on the shelves, and in the cupboards lay piled his old comic books and Tintins, and a pair of sandals. She pulled back the curtains which were drawn at night for no particular reason by Jochna before she went home. Meanwhile, Mini had settled into an arm-chair in the hall, and was already studying a very funny book by Bonophul, peering hard at the print through her glasses. As if out of some vestigial survival of embarrassment, Nando rose from the carpet, dragging his blanket behind him, a dark four-foot-ten-inch demon, and walked dolefully towards the kitchen.

Khuku sat down on the arm-chair next to Mini, who closed her book and looked up.

'How are you feeling, Mini?' asked Khuku. 'Did you sleep well last night?'

'I'm much better already,' she said. 'Your house is so beautiful and comfortable that I have no choice but to feel better!' She laughed as she always did, her dark brown lips parting to reveal her uneven white teeth, her head and shoulders and chest shaking together. Then, almost immediately, the sides of her eyes crinkled shyly, because she was one of those who had grown up in an age when it was believed that to laugh too hard was not proper for a woman. 'In fact,' she said, 'the moment I'm better I'll be going back. There will be a lot of school-work this term.'

'Quiet!' said Khuku. 'I can't ask you something without you talking about going back! Will you let yourself rest for a while?'

'There is Shantidi,' murmured Mini.

'Shantidi is capable of taking care of herself!' said Khuku. 'She travels from one end of the city to the other!'

'She might get into a bad mood...' said Mini softly, staring at the carpet.

'Shantidi,' said Khuku gently, 'is very anxious that you get better. She'll be unhappy if you go back before you are perfectly all right.'

Mini began to laugh again, this time pursing her lips and nodding her head slowly backward and forward. It was not clear why – probably at Khuku's childish insistence, or probably because she could not picture Shantidi unhappy; a little bad tempered, yes, if she could not find her sandesh mould or a hairpin. Only five days ago, when Khuku had arrived in her Ambassador to pick up Mini from where she and her older sister lived in North Calcutta, in the New Municipal Corporation Building,

4

which was, in fact, twenty-five years old, Shantidi had been away at an acquaintance's funeral. Three years ago, recovering from hepatitis, she had gone about, somewhat tardily, with a torch and a walking-stick. Now she did not fear even trams and buses, and pushed her way inside and pushed her way outside. When Khuku was helping Mini down the dark stairs towards her car, Shantidi, after expressing her grief to a relative, and saying with all conviction what a wonderful person was the departed, a simple and pure-hearted woman who had never harmed anyone, was eating jilepi and shingara from a paper plate, and talking about her favourite subject, politics. The caterers, in another room, were heating food in drums over open fires, and stirring the hot and bubbling mass with long black khuntis. The dead one had led a long and peaceful life, and how wonderful it was, thought Shantidi to herself, that her daughter's eyes, who was smilingly welcoming guests, followed everywhere by her small inquisitive son, should still be a little red with weeping.

Now, at six in the morning, in a house on Ishwar Chandra Vidyasagar Road, a very dark twenty-eight-year-old man was hiding, terrified, beneath his blankets. What he was terrified of was not clear, but he had slipped under the blanket as far as he could, and only his frowning eyes, his forehead, and his hair, the shorter ones of which stuck out like rays and stings in every direction, were visible. Almost everyone was awake, moving in that dreary somnolent state from wash-basin to toilet to wash-basin, except the young man. His father – Khuku's brother – who, wearing a pullover and tennis shoes, had just returned from a walk by the lake, was now climbing the stairs, singing, and hesitating between one step and the next to repeat a particular note till he rendered it as he desired. With a grunt of finality, Bhaskar threw off, in a storm, the blanket and sat upright. Then, as if he were some kind of new-born animal, he propelled himself on his bottom to the edge of the bed, his legs sticking out before him like two huge talons. 'Haridasi,' he shouted. 'Bring tea!' Is that Bhaskar? thought his mother, downstairs. Though fourteen years had passed since his voice had changed to a man's voice, a tenth of a moment always elapsed before his mother adjusted herself to her son's grown-upness. Without a word, standing by the edge of the bed, Bhaskar began to do a quick, abbreviated version of his exercises, recommended to him by a physiotherapist for his back-ache, breathing in quickly, bending hurriedly to clutch his knees, as if they were about to desert him, and then expiring in relief. Piyu, his sister, supporting her weight on one leg, was brushing her teeth furiously and rhythmically, and observing him closely; she had been standing there and brushing for a full minute, till her teeth had been lost for the Colgate foam forming at her mouth.

'Dash oh do yoo ayi goo,' she said.

'What?' said Bhaskar, looking sideways from his ostrich posture, his head hanging between his knees.

She went to the wash-basin and spat, and then rinsed her mouth thoroughly, blowing her left cheek first and then her right. Returning, she repeated:

'That won't do you any good.'

'You mind your own business,' said Bhaskar, and bent down again.

She went away, hurt. And when his conscience was satisfied, Bhaskar rushed to the alna and began to look for his jeans among the silently hanging clothes. 'Where is it, where is it?' but the clothes would give no answer. Then he found them and wore them hurriedly, clamping his lower lip with his teeth as he strove to push a button through a button-hole, but zipping the fly effortlessly. He slipped off his crumpled kurta and put on a pink one. A children's song was coming from the radio in the next house: 'Sajalpurer kaajal meye naite nemechhe,' sung in a ringing, girlish voice. From the walls above the faces of his mother's parents gazed at him, she with the sari's aanchal draped about her head and smiling slightly, he serious and patriarchal in a white kurta, his skin even darker than Bhaskar's. Morning came to the house through the windows at the back of the second storey, via a school in a field and a doctor's house; when a shutter was opened, the light found its way straight to one's eye. By this time mynahs, shaliks, sparrows, crows, had begun to echo on parapets and window-sills, and a cat had woken up and fallen asleep again.

The doorbell rang, and Bhaskar's mother wiped her brow with her sari and proceeded towards the veranda. Looking past the branches of the shajana tree, she saw Mohit between their gaps, no longer wearing shorts, but trousers, standing with his bicycle on the pavement. Four days ago he had completed his end-of-term exams, for which he used to study alone early in the mornings. Today, he had woken up at five as usual, had a bath, wished his mother goodbye, and come cycling to Vidyasagar Road.

'Ei, Mohit! What do you want?'

'What do you mean, what do I want?'

'You want to come in?'

Mohit stood with one hand on the bicycle. The road was misty behind him.

'Yes, I want to come in,' he said sternly.

'Wait there,' said his great-aunt, and wandered inside, smiling. 'Haridasi!' she called.

'Yes ma,' came the small, childish voice from the kitchen.

'Open the door outside for Mohit.'

A minute later, coming up the stairs, Mohit found Piyu standing on the first-floor landing.

'How was the ride?' she asked. After Mohit had grown an inch last year he was as tall as her and could look her in the eye.

'Fantastic! I came through the lake.'

His great-aunt began to follow him around like a mendicant.

'Will you have luchi, Mohit?' she asked.

'No,' he said.

'Omelette?'

'No.'

'Pithha? Have a pithha. I made them yesterday.'

'No,' said Mohit firmly, as if he were used to warding off such requests. 'In fact, I just had something before I came here.' His hair was still gleaming from the bath he had had half an hour ago.

'What did you have?'

'Oof! What a question,' said Mohit, looking ashamed. 'Milk and toast and roshogolla,' he admitted with a mixture of bravado and embarrassment.

'Would you like a cup of tea?' asked Piyu.

Mohit hesitated; for it was a sign of adulthood to drink tea, and he was tempted, in his great-uncle's house, to partake of a pleasure denied him by his mother.

'All right!' he said impatiently, not looking at anyone in particular. 'All right, I'll have tea!'

When Bhaskar came into the dining-room in his jeans

and pink kurta, tea was still brewing in the pan. Mohit was discussing irrelevancies with his great-aunt and Piyu, his elbows resting on the table, his legs locked around one of the legs of the dining-table. So secure did he look that it seemed no buffeting of fate could move him from his place. Pigeons, in a mire of feathers and excrement, had begun to make crowded noises in a dark foot-wide corridor by the water tank of the next house, which was perpetually visible from the window next to Mohit. But Bhaskar first entered the kitchen and said resentfully:

'Half an hour and you still haven't made it! Dhur – now I don't want it.'

Poor eleven-year-old Haridasi, she took everything literally; her mouth curved downward. She stood on tiptoe and strained to gaze at the pan.

'What could I do?' she said softly. 'I had to open the door for Mohitda.' She said, 'Don't go, Bhaskarda, it'll be ready in a minute.' The smell of tea, strong and bitter-sweet and a little rancid, like sweat, had begun to waft through the kitchen.

But Bhaskar had, without pause, already walked out of the dining-room, saying, 'I'll be back in an hour.' Piyu, still hurt from his retort ten minutes ago, decided she had not heard this. 'What about your tea?' called out his mother. When he did not answer she said to the table, 'Let him do what he likes.' Piyu lifted herself from this scene as if it did not matter. Then Mohit disrupted the small dining-table community further by getting up and shouting, 'Bhaskarmama, wait for me, I'm coming.' 'Ei, where are *you* going?' asked Piyu in astonishment. Deserting them, he revealed, 'With Bhaskarmama!' Bhaskar's father had emerged absent-mindedly from the toilet and was washing his hands with a piece of Lifebuoy soap.

'Where are you going?' he asked. Running down the stairs, Mohit said, 'With Bhaskarmama!'

––––––

When Mohit caught up with him on the pavement, he said: 'Bhaskarmama, I'm coming too.'

Bhaskar put an arm around the boy, who was a little out of breath, and said, 'Then come; I don't mind.' Two pigeons, making rapid pistol-like sounds with their wings, took off over their heads.

Now, at half-past six, two state transport buses went down Ishwar Chandra Vidyasagar Road, blowing their loud hooting horns; they were half empty, an unusual sight. There was a small encampment of rickshaws along part of the pavement, their extended arms planted on the ground, their collapsible roofs raised, their wheels at rest; rickshaw-wallahs, heads and shoulders covered with a piece of cloth, were slapping their hands in imitation of applause and hurling tobacco into their mouths. Retired men, as free as children, all of them dressed for some reason in white dhuti and kurta, were either creeping out of their houses or returning from a walk, with or without a walking-stick. The first to go about their business were the crows, clamorous, a little neurotic, turning up, as usual, by the tea-shop entrance (if one could call that absence in the wall an entrance), by the lane's rubbish dump, on the pavement, upon the roofs. Fog, a compound of charcoal smoke, exhaust fumes, and mist, hung in the lanes; you did not notice it at close quarters, but, a little distance away, you saw it loitering by balconies and doorways. The colours of the houses on Vidyasagar Road, pink, or moss green, or light yellow or blue, were dimmed by the mist, till they looked like the colour of old cotton saris that have been worn for many years and still not thrown away.

They came to a house. An old man was sitting on the balcony of the first floor upon a wicker stool and eating from a bowl. A woman in a cardigan leaned over the banister and looked over her shoulder and cried, 'Hurry up, Mira, do you want to miss your bus?' The old man dipped his spoon into the bowl and said, 'Don't scold her, ma, she's a little slow.' The mother said, 'Mira – Mira? I can see the bus coming now,' although the lane was still empty. The door to the room on the ground floor was open, separated from the courtyard by a porch which was a little stage that accommodated a coir mat and two or three pairs of rubber slippers. There was a message on the wall outside: C.P.I.(M.) FOR UNITY AND HAR-MONY AMONG ALL COMMUNITIES. A man, wearing pyjamas, a shirt, and a sleeveless pullover, came to the door and said: 'You're late.' 'Give it to me, don't waste time,' said Bhaskar. As they were waiting, Bhaskar lit a cigarette, and Mohit, still a little awed and shocked by this act, began to pace up and down the porch, stopping only to inspect a fern that had grown on one side. A small girl had arrived at the pavement in uniform, a blue skirt, white shirt, and blue pullover, accompanied by a servant girl who would herself have been no more than ten years old. She was swinging her plastic water bottle upon its infinitely co-operative strap and standing a little way from the servant girl and talking to herself. Occasionally, she looked up at where her mother and possibly her grand-father were standing, ignoring the rest of the world, as if her imminent farewell were meant only for them. The man in the sleeveless pullover emerged with a pile of

Ganashakti and transferred it from his arms to Bhaskar's. 'Did you sleep well last night?' he said sourly. Bhaskar ground the cigarette underfoot and kicked it into the courtyard among the mournful plants and ash-grey earth. 'I'll see you later,' he replied. He walked out of the gate, followed hotly by Mohit.

Each newspaper was folded and tied with a jute string. 'You take half,' said Bhaskar. 'Here.' 'What are you going to do with them?' asked Mohit, cradling them and laughing. 'Distribute some,' revealed Bhaskar very seriously, 'and sell the others later.' Bundled up, they were slim and surprisingly hard, and each paper could be held in the fist like a baton. They began to walk back the way they had come, to an increasing accompaniment of noise from motorcycles and cars. As they passed the houses, Bhaskar aimed his paper at one or two of the porches, where it fell on the floor with a sharp sound, or sent it flying at a first-storey balcony, a swift journey in the course of which the paper arched in mid air and finally landed just beyond the flower-pots. There was a special purpose in these throws, for the readers of *Ganashakti* were fellow-travellers of the Communist Party, they believed in its necessity and its vision, and an inexplicable bond was formed between the distributor, whose every aim with the bundle seemed to be a salute, and the silent house. Mohit glanced back to see if the houses in which the readers of *Ganashakti* lived were any different from the others, but they were the same, with the fronts of balconies and doors painted in white or green, and other parts chipping away to reveal a structure of stone and iron that was as intricate and fragile as a honeycomb. The two went on until Bhaskar had completed the round and they had come to the end of Vidyasagar Road. By now Bhaskar had acquired a small limp; Mohit said: 'You're growing old, Bhaskarmama. The Party must be in a bad way if they're taking members like you.' 'What do you think I should do?' 'I think you should do yoga,' said Mohit. 'Buy a book and learn the asanas. Or you won't be selling newspapers for long.' 'I want to have some tea,' said Bhaskar.

AFTERNOON SAW Khuku and Mini fall asleep on the double bed, Mini on the side on which Shib slept at night. These days the fan was not switched on, and the women hugged their own bodies, a light shawl lying casually upon their feet, taking on their tender, ghostly shape, while now and then Khuku complained of the cold and shivered. She had had all the windows closed except one, which let in a smell of smoke that must have drifted, unmoored, from a distance. Because the room, without the hum and movement of the fan, was so still, the world outside seemed proportionately larger, with more space having come into existence to accommodate the different afternoon noises, of bird call and bird chatter, and vendors, hammering, and taxis. Somewhere below, cars arrived, people got out, doors were slammed one by one, or almost together: not everyone was asleep. Next to Khuku, Mini, very softly, was snoring, and on another floor, someone coughed, the little angry explosions seeming to go off just outside the window. Khuku clasped her throat with her hand and warmed it. How pleasing that sensation was, warmth, so rarely known for most of the year! Khuku began to fall asleep.

Outside, Jochna, sitting on the veranda at the end of the hall, combed her loose wet hair and considered the

city. Uma, leaning over the banister and looking unconsciously upon the tiny heads of the watchmen far below,
hung clothes to dry from different-coloured plastic clips.
In a slow, imperceptible way, the city swam around her,
the temple with its pseudo-classical shape that was being
'completed' for fifteen years, which they thought of simply
as 'the temple', the vacant white perfect terraces of
decaying ancestral mansions, surrounded by the enigmatic
tops of masses of trees, the solitary, invisible factory
chimney, with its waving plume of smoke the colour of
pigeon feathers, the weathered white marble dome of an
ancient princely house now given out to wedding parties,
shining as coldly and beautifully as a planet, and, at large
intervals, the famous multi-storeyed buildings with mythical Sanskrit names, all this swam around the two maidservants, Uma and Jochna, the first, who did not know her
age, but looked thirty years old, abandoned by her husband, but vermilion still fresh and bright and new each
day in the parting of her hair, and the other, fourteen
years old, short, dark, with intelligent eyes, and slow to
smile. Uma was telling her the story yet again:

'He begins to go for weeks to the other village, until I
ask him, "What do you do there?" and he tells me, "I'm
living with my wife," and I say to him, "If she is your
wife then who am I, eh?" He was like that from the first
day, I can touch you and say that. He said, "I never
wanted to marry you, it was my people who made me."'

Jochna had other stories to tell, of her elder sister who
was learning to make clothes in a tailoring class, and her
nine-year-old brother who went to a municipal school.
Tinkling sounds came from outside, of hammering and
chiselling, as labourers worked like bees, and seven- or
eight-storeyed buildings rose in the place of ancestral

mansions that had been razed cruelly to the ground, climbing up like ladders through screens of dust. An old mansion opposite the veranda had been repainted white, to its last banister and pillar, so that it looked like a set of new teeth. In the lawn before it, a mali in khaki shorts, alone, unaware of being watched, fussed over a row of potted plants. In another sphere altogether, birds took off from a tree or parapet, or the roof of some rich Marwari's house, startling and speckling the neutral sky. Not a moment was still or like another moment. In a window in a servants' outhouse attached to a mansion – both the master's house and the servants' lost in a bond now anachronistic and buried – a light shone even at this time of the day, beacon of winter.

For a long time, neither of them seemed to move from where they were sitting. Then, burrowing into the hall, they lay down on the carpet between two chairs, a sofa, and a centre table, their feet, or Uma's shoulder, visible depending from where one saw them, leaving empty the place where they had been, a veranda framing a winter sky, and light, an occasional sweep of birds, and grey, thinning smoke. Now only the sounds remained, giving a sense of the city outside, caught in the light, and a mosquito, like a lost aeroplane, that had wandered in; the sound of the two voices, Jochna's and Uma's, fell like drops of water, again, and again, deep, sounding muffled underneath the sofa. The colour of Jochna's dress, with red and black flowers, reminded one of the interiors of pavement stalls on Rashbehari Avenue, with dresses folded or hung up in the afternoon, and a fist clutching forty rupees. It could have been worn by a small plastic doll. There was something of a cat's secrecy about the two figures.

In the kitchen, the blue fluorescent light was suddenly extinguished, leaving its doorway dark until a pale, undecided patch of colour appeared in it – Nando, in his white pyjamas and shirt. On his black face, the eyebrows were knitted, either because he could not see well these days, or out of concern or puzzlement over some elusive thing.

'Hey, you,' he said.

The two figures stirred as if they had been immersed in something, lifting their heads like cats raising their whiskers from a bowl of milk.

'What?' said Jochna, altering her voice to a surprising hardness and volume, for she, among the two, was unafraid of his bully and bravado.

Nando softened.

'What?' he returned.

'What are you saying?' said Jochna.

'No, I was only saying – have you washed the pans?'

'Can't you see?' She might have been addressing a hectoring child.

Nando didn't mind this scolding. As if something had suddenly occurred to him, he turned back to the kitchen. Poor man, he had probably just wanted to have a few words before going in and smoking his bidi by himself in the servant's room – because he never slept during the day. But the girls kept him out of their afternoon world, to which they had already returned, their sides and shoulders pressed against the carpet till they hurt, their breasts rising and falling lightly. They let no one encroach upon their territory between the sofa and the centre table; if someone did, they got up, flustered and serious. And Nando could not make normal conversation. He either flirted with Uma, standing beside her by the kitchen basin and brushing his shoulder against hers, or they quarrelled loudly, or made fun of each other in small, irritating, uncharitable ways. With Jochna he dared nothing at all, because she bore his daughter's name, and was just as short with him as his daughter was; in fact he tried to please her whenever he could; but, in that frail demonic body with red eyes and tobacco-stained hands, there also existed a genuine paternal soft spot for Jochna. This was known and accepted in the household.

While these people rested at home, Khuku's husband sat in an office on the outskirts of the city. It was an old company, once reputable and British owned, called Little's, and it produced sweets and chocolates. There was a time when its oval tin – Little's Magic Assortment – was available in every shop in Calcutta, and its toffees and lozenges in cellophane wrappers stored in jars in every cigarette shop. The company had changed hands several times, until now it was owned by the state government, and, after having made losses for many years, was named a 'sick unit'. Its loyal machines still produced, poignantly, myriads of perfectly shaped toffees, but that organ of the company that was responsible for distribution had for long been lying numb and dysfunctional, so that the toffees never quite reached the retailer's shelves. Years of labour problems had sapped the factory and its adjoining offices of impetus, but ever since the Communist Party came to power, the atmosphere had changed to a benign, co-operative inactivity, with a cheerful trade unionism replacing the tensions of the past, the representatives of the chocolate company now also representing the government and the party, and the whole thing becoming a relaxed, ungrudging family affair. This kind of company was not rare in the 'public sector'; in fact, brave little bands of men held out in such islands everywhere; but

Khuku's husband, before retiring, had worked in a successful private company, where every department whirred and ticked from nine to five thirty like clockwork, and he and his colleagues had only heard of the renegade lives of the 'public sector' companies from the outside. They were spoken of as backward but colourful tribes with a time-tested culture of tea-drinking, gossip, and procrastination, who had stoutly defended, for many years, their modes of communion and exchange from being taken over by an alien 'work ethic'. Little did he know, then, that, in his days of retirement, he too would end up here. It was, in a sense, a relaxing place to be in, like withdrawing to some outpost that was cut off from the larger movements of the world. The factory was tucked away in a lane on the outskirts, not far from an important and congested junction on the main road, where no one would have expected it, hidden behind stone walls and a huge rusting gate that opened reluctantly to outsiders. Once, the two-storeyed buildings made of red brick, with long continuous corridors and verandas, with arches that were meant to give shelter from the tropical heat, would have been impressive and even grand. Now it was like a hostel; cups of tea travelled from room to room, and bearers ran back and forth in the verandas. There was a perpetual air of murmuring intrigue, the only sign of life, until the doors and windows were shut in the evening.

Yet the employees were, in their own way, simple and good-hearted. And though Khuku's husband was only an adviser, they treated him with a bit of extra respect and sometimes as if he ran the place. 'Put it back on the rails, sir,' they said, 'we need people like you. What a state the company's in!' And Khuku's husband came home and told Khuku these stories, his eyes shining, and felt young again. And Khuku told her brother in Vidyasagar Road, 'He'll put the company right.' Khuku's brother, in a kind of infatuated haze, said, 'Little's – Little's will be all right again.' For many days after, he would not let Piyu or his brother's children touch Cadbury, and go out himself in search of Little's chocolates. His relationship would become temporarily strained with the keeper of the local shop, Pick and Choose, who was always doing his accounts on a scrap of paper and was not very concerned about human beings. 'What, sir, you don't keep Little's toffees – *we* ate it when *we* were young. *You* must have eaten it as well. No, this shop is not what it used to be,' he would conclude, shaking his head. 'What can we do, Bhola babu?' the shopkeeper would say. 'They don't *send* us the chocolates,' as if he were speaking of a powerful but heartless family.

Meanwhile, Khuku's husband had discovered that, in spite of their good intentions, the employees, after making their supportive and rallying statements, went back first thing to a convivial round of tea in the canteen. So he resorted to saying, 'Do it at once!' or 'I want some order in this place!' till he knew better. A few weeks later, he met, at last, the Managing Director. The Managing Director had joined the company three months ago, but since he was a state civil servant as well, he naturally could not spend all his time here – he was merely a stop-gap before a full-time man came along. 'Pleased to meet you, Mr Purakayastha,' he said to Khuku's husband. 'I've heard so much about you – we are very fortunate, very fortunate. We need your skills, sir. Tell me – are you happy with your office?' A new room had been refurnished specially for him, with a filing cabinet, a telephone, and a window that looked out over the wall into the lane. 'Oh yes, you shouldn't have gone through the trouble,' said Khuku's husband. 'No *trouble*, no trouble at all! In fact, you're the one that's going through the trouble,' he said, waving around him. 'No, no,' said Khuku's husband. 'In fact, Mr Sengupta, I would like to have a talk with you.' He smiled and looked seriously at the other. 'Definitely, Mr Purakayastha. We are very keen to hear what you have to say. Definitely.' Yet the Managing Director – a relatively young man – spoke like one who would not be around for long, for all Managing Directors used this company as a kind of airport lounge, from where they went on to somewhere else, never to be seen again. And so it was the eager tea-drinking employees that Khuku's husband spent most afternoons with.

'**R**EALLY? Are you sure?'

It was morning again. Khuku was speaking to Mohit's mother, Puti, in their familiar East Bengali dialect.

'Mohit told me yesterday.'

Khuku laughed, disarmed by the picture that composed itself before her eyes – Bhaskar marching down the street early in the morning, brandishing newspapers.

'What will he do next?' she said.

'He should get married before he does anything.'

'I hear they're trying to find a girl.'

'It won't be easy.'

'Oh, it won't be easy, will it?' she asked.

She cradled the receiver and curled her toes; her feet were up on the divan.

'Mashi, how can it be easy?' cried Puti. Her voice came agitated but musical on the ear-piece. 'You know how long Arun took to find a wife.'

'Yes, Arun,' agreed Khuku. 'But Arun is so … short.'

'Arun is short but Bhaskar is dark,' said Puti. 'And tell me, which father will give away his daughter to a boy who has Party connections?'

'Which father will?' echoed Khuku. 'It's Bhola's fault. Though he's a good-looking boy in his way. I used to call him "Black Beauty" when he was younger.'

'Leave your "Black Beauty",' said Puti. '"Black Beauty" won't help him when his father-in-law finds he sells *Ganashakti*.'

———

Later, Khuku put her feet in her slippers and walked to the dining-table. Mini was wrapped in a shawl, and Khuku's husband was wearing a dark blue slip-over upon a shirt whose sleeves were rolled up above his wrists.

'It's cold,' said Khuku, pulling her shawl tightly around her shoulders.

Both hers and Mini's hair were tied in buns at the back; both had wavy hair, but Khuku's was crowded with curls, with not an inch of straightness to be found anywhere, only skips and jumps and leaps.

'Yes,' said Mini. 'Ever since yesterday.'

'You should wear your full-sleeve pullover,' said Khuku to her husband.

'Where is it?' he asked, a little crossly but dreamily.

'Can't you find anything? Mini,' she said, 'he really can't do anything for himself, and, God forbid, if I die before he does...'

Mini smiled at her friend.

'Have some oranges,' said Khuku to Mini. 'They're sweet as sugar. Mritunjoy bought them yesterday from Park Circus, and do you know how much they cost – you won't believe me – fourteen rupees a dozen.'

'What are you saying?' said Mini, looking up.

'Yes – fourteen rupees a dozen! Who said Calcutta is not an expensive city? They say that Bombay is expensive, but I think Calcutta is no less.' She said this as a complaint but a note of pride was audible in her voice.

'Jochna!' she cried. 'Give Didimoni an orange! No, don't give it, bring the bowl here, I'll choose one myself.' Jochna, with a mysterious smile on her face, held the bowl in her hands while Khuku delved in a hugely absorbed way into the oranges, turning them over, till she picked one and handed it to Jochna. 'Give it to Didimoni,' she said.

'Give one to Shib,' murmured Mini.

She looked at her husband, as if she had just noticed him.

'Will you have one?' she said.

He shook his head, never wasting a word if he didn't have to. As Mini, with her small dark fingers, ripped the peel, the smell of orange suddenly burst upon the air.

'Do you know what Puti told me?' Khuku separated the portions of the orange, which came off with white threads hanging by their sides like bits of cobweb. Absent-mindedly she picked off some of the threads with her finger and put a piece in her mouth. 'Bhaskar sells *Ganashakti* in the morning. Mmm, it's like sugar.' She picked up another piece and sprinkled sweet white powder upon it. 'The sweeter the better,' she said. Such a sweet tooth had she that when she was a girl she would eat handfuls of sugar, crunching the large unrefined crystals happily with her molars, and no one would notice, for she was a lonely child who haunted the margins of her large family. Once she had eaten sweet homoeopathic pills till they had given her a stomach-ache, much to the disgust of her elder sister. What was normally called 'food' had held no appeal for her until she got married.

'*Ganashakti?*' said Khuku's husband.

'Yes,' said Khuku, spitting out the pips into her cupped hands. 'Mohit was there with him.'

Khuku's husband shook his head, but said nothing.

'There are many boys in my area,' said Mini, putting a piece of orange in her mouth, 'who get so involved they don't do anything else for the rest of their lives. Many. Two boys, Anshuman Biswas and Partho Guha – good students at school – have even left their jobs.' Khuku and Mini worked busily while talking, spitting out pips which were being heaped in torn pieces of the peel. They were enjoying the winter.

WHEN AFTERNOON came to Vidyasagar Road, wet clothes – Piyu's dresses, Bhaskar's pyjamas and kurtas, even a few soggy towels – hung from a clothes-line which stretched from one side to another on the veranda of the first floor. The line, which had not been tightly drawn anyway, sagged with the pressure of the heavy wet clothes that dripped, from sleeves and trouser-ends, a curious grey water on to the floor, and, especially in the middle, one noticed the line curved downward, as if a smile were forming. To the people in the house, the clothes formed a screen or curtain which threw shadows and provided bewitching glimpses of the speedy criss-crosses of the grill, and through those criss-crosses bits of the balcony of the house opposite and the sky and the shajana tree, all of which surprised by still being there. The slow leaking of the drops of water from the clothes and their casual, flirtatious flutter with every breeze would not have been noticed by the passer-by on the road, who, if he had looked beyond the remaining leaves on the shajana tree and the iron nerve-pattern of the grill, would have seen them suspended there stilly, like ghosts or patches of colour. Who had put them there? To know that, one would have had to be present at half-past two, when Haridasi, helped by Bhaskar's mother, watched regally by Piyu, had hung up the clothes one by one, till the passer-by would have seen all the figures, including Piyu in the doorway, gradually consumed by the clothes that they were hanging up.

Winter came only once a year, and it changed the city. It gave its people, as they wore their sweaters and mufflers, a sense of having gone somewhere else, the slight sense of the wonder and dislocation of being in a foreign city. Even the everyday view from their own houses was a little strange. Smoke travelled everywhere, robbing the sunlight of its fire. Afternoon, with its gentle orange-yellow light, was the warmest time of day, though the wet clothes, assisted by a breeze, dried more slowly than in the summer. And as the orange light fell on the brickwork and the sides of the houses, it was easier to tell, from the flushed rose centre that now appeared on a terrace and now a parapet, that its origins lay in fire.

On the street, Tommy the dog haunted the rubbish-heap again, probing, in a concerned way, its bright smelly edges with his nozzle. When someone cranked the handle of the tube-well, it creaked and twanged like a one-string instrument. Crows, sometimes alighting on a window-sill or a banister, clamoured as usual, comforting the child in every human figure in the house, those who were half asleep or awake, bringing up memories of other human, beloved faces, or creating the expectation of homecomings. Their cries had something to do with hope and return and the continuance of human business. Bhaskar's mother, turning in her sleep, grew full with the return of her son in the evening.

She was sleeping with Piyu on the bed; her husband lay sleeping on the divan in the next room. He was snoring, but gently compared to his night-time snores, so that one would not have heard it from the bed that Piyu and her mother were sleeping on, but, moving closer to the doorway, one might have been distracted by a far-away sound that was hardly a sound at all, trapped, urgent, but private. Then, abruptly, one would have realized what it was, and the body with its small belly and bald patch, clothed in kurta and pyjamas, and the frowning mouth and big nose, would have formed around the snore.

On Bhaskar's mother's outstretched hand, on the shining dark brown skin, there was, near the thumb and the index finger, a large pink spot like a rose where the skin had peeled off after one drop of boiling oil had leapt on it while she was frying luchis. The yellow Burnol paste that she put there timidly and perfunctorily after stubborn exhortations from Piyu had now faded into what looked like healing dabs of turmeric. She was dark, and slept intensely, while Piyu, beside her, was fair and fresh-faced, a plant that had been nurtured in this garden, in the shadow of pillows, cupboards, shelves, clothes-horses, untouched as yet by life. Let it always be so, the house around her seemed to say, the four walls and the beam on the ceiling, let us always keep her as she is. Let her not leave us. She breathed gently. The sun came in through the clothes-line and printed the wall and the blue bed-cover with triangles and rectangles.

Haridasi, small Haridasi, barely four feet six inches tall, had cleared the dining-table, first cupping her endlessly compliant palm and pushing bits of moist rice and salt that had littered the table into its dark cave, to rest there between her heart line and her life line, collecting bits of fishbone as well to deposit them there, and then curling her fingers as if she were holding a secret and throwing the debris into the kitchen basin, though she had been told not to. She wiped the table after this with a wet cloth. Then she sat in one corner of the kitchen, the only one awake in the house, a guest, a stranger, a friend, and ate from a plate with a heap of rice and a puddle of dal and vegetables on one side. She was quiet as a mouse. Without being aware of it, she tried to mix the puddle of dal uniformly with the huge quantity of rice. She loved rice.

It was today, in the evening, that Bhaskar's mother would take her husband to the doctor for his annual check-up. For about two weeks she had been persuading him to go, but something else always came up instead. Now, at last, they had a free evening ahead of them. It was a short journey by car, past the Lake Market in Rashbehari Avenue, turning into a lane at whose entrance wheat and grain were piled in open heaps by the roadside. It was a lane they came to seldom, except on these visits to the doctor's chambers, and they usually forgot where exactly the house was, with its porch lit by one bulb and the narrow corridor, smoke-filled in the winter, that ran next to it, inward to the green waiting-room at the back. The lane seemed far away and strange, and yet, in reality, was only a short distance from Khuku's house, and from the lane in which Bhaskar's mother's sister lived, and Piyu's college, and Lake Market where, once or twice a week, Bhaskar's mother bought fish and vegetables. Once the visit was over they immediately went to the Fern Road Pharmacy and bought the medicines that had been prescribed, and proceeded without further delay to a relative's house.

Bhaskar's father had a great, childlike respect for this doctor. Though he was himself an engineer, the doctor was what in his youth some of the brightest young men went on to be: an FRCP from London. Those were the days when young men went to England, not America, and came back with degrees and sometimes even an English wife who wore a sari. The letters FRCP made Bhaskar's father feel that both he and India were suddenly, completely, though temporarily, young again. Each time he went there, he signed his name on the compounder's slip and sat in the waiting room with his wife and the other patients as shyly as if he were visiting his in-laws, flicking through, meanwhile, old copies of *Span*. Once they were inside, he loved listening to the doctor's diagnosis and asking questions about the prescription, not because he doubted the doctor but because he always wished, whenever he had the opportunity, to widen his own limited, though not negligible, knowledge of medicine. The doctor was a mild, slightly boring man whom time had passed by; he wore black-framed bifocal spectacles and had small tufts of black and grey hair coming out of his ears. He was content to see fewer patients these days and sit behind his old wooden table with its green leather top, his arms resting behind a glass paperweight with little flecks of pink and blue suspended in its strange, crystalline atmosphere, and talk in a leisurely way about his son who was studying at Caltech, and in winter, about all the marriages that were now underway in the city. Behind him, on the wall, there were two framed photographs – the class of '49 in Calcutta Medical College, and the class of '55 in London, the students mostly men, with recent, smart, close-cropped hair-cuts.

Now an interminable mail-train passed on the railway tracks that formed the horizon that could be seen in the gap between the houses on the other side of Vidyasagar

Road. For a while, all other local and habitual noises, of birds and cars, were subsumed under the long, swelling note of the mail-train whistle, which, with its lone trumpeting, made the air vibrate around one. But yet they slept in that vibrating air. Then, when the train had gone, the air was cleansed, and the room was as quiet as its reflection in the dressing-table mirror, with Oil of Ulay, Lactocalamine, Vaseline, Pond's Dream Flower Talc, and two lipsticks arranged carefully, with all devotion and seriousness, on the shelf before it. Very slowly, like town officials who had respectfully ceased their transactions for a minute, the crows and sparrows began again, but sounding more distant now, even chastized, perhaps in comparison to the grand interlude of the train whistle. In this new, petty, semi-silent, post-whistle moment came the postman to Vidyasagar Road, dressed in civilian clothes, a dark red sweater, a full-sleeve shirt whose broad collars were hidden by the sweater's neck, and black terrycotton trousers with bottoms that were wide and floppy; on his shoulder there was a hand-woven cotton sling bag such as college students swing casually and thoughtlessly by their sides, crammed with neat, though uneven, stairways of letters, a small blue aerogramme climbing up to a broad brown-paper envelope, which rose again to a disproportionately small inland postcard. This frail man, eclipsed almost entirely by his sweater and his trousers, now, retrieving more and more piles from his shoulder-bag, seemed the paradigm of modest, unattractive, but real generosity, as he, without any special demonstrativeness or affection, left at least one letter in every letter-box on his progress from one house to another. In the yellow-green letter-box by the gate to Bhaskar's house there came a wedding card with 'Shubho Bibaho' inscribed on the envelope; on the card inside, embossed in fine gold lines on a red background, a wedding procession moved forward, looking as wedding processions might once have looked, with a palanquin and red and gold revellers in profile, wearing turbans and blowing pipes and beating drums and making an infernal racket. There was another card, announcing a funeral, with 'Ganga' printed in Bengali on the envelope. Lying on it was a yellow post-card from Bangladesh, sent by a distant relative; one half of the square, divided by a vertical line from the other, had clean horizontal lines that had been meticulously loaded with Bhaskar's father's name and his address, and the numbers of the pin code imprisoned inside tiny printed boxes. The letter, written in blue ink, began on this side with pleasantries and general reminiscences and then came, in its tidy persistent way, to occupy all of the other side, ending with a plea for financial help for a daughter's marriage. Like a house which shelters sons, daughters, grandparents, servants, frustrations, expecta-tions, a whole world under its roof, the postcard, with not one inch of it wasted, gave whatever space it could to words that expressed both necessary sentiments and urgent requirements. And there was a letter from Robi, a nephew in Pennsylvania, with photographs of his daugh-ter enclosed, now seven. He had once lived in this house as a student. The one-dollar postage stamp, with Lincoln's picture on it, would be acquired by Mohit for his collection.

On the first floor of the house, on the double bed where Piyu and her mother were now sleeping, a grand-mother had lived twenty years ago. She was Bhaskar's father's mother; of her seven children, Khuku was her favourite, but she was in those days in Bombay with her husband and a son of her own. From time to time, the grandmother's children, who were scattered with their families in different parts of India, would visit this house to see their mother, who was eccentric and did not have much to say to them any more; she had brought them up and now her duties, she had decided, were over. Bhaskar's father, Bhola, and Khuku, who was only a year older than him, often called their mother 'Goonga'. The bed on which Piyu and her mother were now sleeping was her bed, her divan, her arm-chair, her footstool. In the morning her quilt and pillows were banked on one side of the bed, the bed beaten with a jhata by Durga, and then draped with a bed-cover. She, wearing her white sari, for her husband had died thirty years ago, sat peering at the *Amrita Bazaar Patrika* through her reading glasses, beginning at the first paragraph on the first page and ending at the last. No one dared bother her but the children, among whom she was only openly affectionate towards Piyu, who could still barely walk, and was regarded by everyone, including six-year-old Bhaskar, as a discovery, a curiosity, and especially amusing in the way she imitated certain grown-up gestures. The grandmother's lunch was laid out on a table before the bed by Nando, who worked then in this house, and looked much the same in his white shirt and pyjamas, his hair oiled, and his face demonlike. 'Ei Nando,' she would shout, 'Bring the salt and the oil!' and Nando would rush back with salt on a plate and a bowl of mustard oil. She had died a few years later. The pomelo tree by her window, whose fruit she ate with mustard oil, secretly adding sugar, had blossomed again this winter, its fruit picked and stolen by a new generation of urchins and scallywags who looked exactly like the ones who had climbed the tree twenty years ago. Some of her children, in those twenty years, had grown old and died as well, leaving Khuku, Bhola, and two more brothers, including the eldest, who, though hunched now, and forgetful of names, still found time to get angry about umpires' decisions in cricket matches.

It was an old house, a hospitable house. In the big room on the second floor, which Bhaskar now had more or less to himself, and where he engaged in animated discussions or restful gossip with comrades from the Party, shy men with moustaches whose frail chests suddenly expanded during these discussions – on the large bed in this room Bhaskar and his brother Manik, who was now in Germany, used to sleep once. When Khuku's son, Bablu, came down for the summer, Khuku's elder sister would also have arrived from the hills of Assam where, in a town with a funny name that sounded like a kitchen utensil, she was head mistress in a girls' school. Reading everything from *Beowulf* to *Puja* annuals at the oddest of angles – for she would lie sideways and let the magazine dangle from the fingers of one outstretched hand, moving grudgingly only when it dawned on her that it was impossible to turn the page without the aid of the hand that was trapped beneath her – reading everything at such angles had given her eye a squint, and her an incongruous lost and searching look. Incongruous, for, despite being widowed when she was thirty-four, she had raised her children robustly, feeding them well and twisting their ears. During those summers, on the bed on the second floor, she told Bablu and Bhaskar and Manik stories about ancient Rome, and the last days of Pompeii. At present, the bed upstairs was empty, with winter sunlight falling upon it, obstructed only by the mullions in the windows, and Bhaskar was away at the factory in

Howrah – but once he had lain there on his stomach with a new book before him and seen rakkhoshes with fangs and nose-rings drink the blood of innocent kings, rakkhoshes who married female rakkhoshes and produced hordes of fearful little khokkhoshes with small fangs and round eyes. Durga had told Bhaskar and Manik when to be careful of ghosts – between two and three o'clock in the afternoon, when grown-ups slept or were away at work and even real objects threw no shadows, and, at night, during the pregnant hours that preceded dusk. If they sensed anything unearthly, Bhaskar and Manik promptly muttered to themselves the lines they knew by heart:

> *Ghoul's my daughter,*
> *Ghost's my son.*
> *Ram's in my heart,*
> *And no harm can be done.*

The children came to the house like guests; their parents and Durga were already there when they arrived. They welcomed them and took them out of their first wondering, semi-conscious state. Once, when Bhaskar was seven and Manik five, they saw from their bed at three or four in the morning a woman who was not Durga or their mother hanging clothes to dry in the bathroom; then they fell asleep again. It was an old house; a family had lived in it before their parents had moved in, and Bhaskar was certain that a woman in that family had died. He hinted, but never admitted, that the woman he and Manik had seen was the same woman.

This house had been a wedding gift from Bhola's father-in-law, part of a dowry. Since then it had gone through changes, for the worse and then for the better, but its red stone floors and stairs and its bottle-green windows with slats and the small prayer-room upstairs had remained the same. The kitchen had been painted; new shelves had been fitted; and the earthen oven, dust-coloured, hollow, into whose sides Durga pushed wood and coal, had been put in the shed at the back of the house where coal and wood used to be kept. Durga herself had returned to her village.

At four o'clock Bhaskar's mother woke as surely as if an alarm clock had gone off inside her. Her eyes, in a face puffed with sleep, opened, red and unfocused. For fifteen years she would get up thus at half-past six in the morning and, with her eyes still small and red, walk towards the bed where Manik and Bhaskar were sleeping and push them by their shoulders, for they always slept on their sides, curled up, one side of their face sunk in the pillow, so that, waking up, their cheeks would be lined with pillow marks. Manik had always been shorter and fairer than Bhaskar, until, when he was fourteen, he shot up and they were both the same height, though Manik, much thinner, sometimes looked taller. And Manik, wandering joyously with his friends in the sun, grew darker, till he was brown as a roasted nut. In the morning, their mother would shake their rather bony frames (Look at them, she would think in disgust, not a bit of flesh on them, just like urchins) and say in a loud whisper, 'Ei, Manik! Ei, Bhaskar! Get up! Get up!' while they clutched their pillows tightly and grew more and more angry in their sleep. When they had any spare time, these two were always arguing and fighting, till, each wrestling titanically with the other, they fell rolling upon the bed. They were separated and brought to their senses by two sharp slaps and smart tugs of the hair administered by their mother. 'You idiots! Look at yourselves! Why don't you fight on the streets? – That's where you should be!' Then she would turn to Bhaskar. 'And you ... I know very well you're the one who starts it ... this other one's an idiot, but you ... you're a mischievous devil!' 'What did I do?' Bhaskar would wail, wiping his eyes and about to cry. 'And look at your face ... Every day it's getting longer, till it's begun to look like a slipper! You don't eat anything, you don't do any work, all you can do is tease this fool!' These days the house was quieter. School had been one of the most difficult of times for everyone, getting up in the morning, coming back in the evening and doing the homework, buying a new white uniform every year, the white shorts being replaced by trousers, Bhaskar, Manik, and Piyu swigging down glasses of Haringhata milk each morning as quickly as if it was medicine, lifting their faces from their glasses with uneven white moustaches around their lips, how their mother suffered for them, what tension, sewing buttons and pushing them towards the school bus on time, the rice still unfinished on their plates – 'Tell him to wait!' Piyu would shout, rinsing her mouth at the basin, 'Tell him to wait!' – while the bus engine rumbled sullenly in the lane; she – their mother – had gone nearly mad coping with it. Yet now the house was silent, lives took shape, things changed, and widened, unused spaces wandered about the house, Manik had gone to Germany, and it seemed there had been a certain innocence and neglect about that time. She wanted to witness it again, she wanted Bhaskar to marry now and have children and that whole maddening bustle to resume.

She got up and walked to the basin and sprinkled her

face with cold water from the tap. She would, before going to the doctor's with her husband, prepare a snack – Chinese noodles with bits of vegetable and perhaps chicken in it – to amuse Piyu and Bhaskar and make herself happy. She called it 'chow mein'. Her husband would demand some, and then finally have to beg for it, but she would deny him the noodles that evening because he was putting on weight and that was bad at his age. Her children would chant 'Chow mein! Chow mein!' as if the name made them hungry and also satisfied their appetites, and if her husband got a small ration upon a plate he would say that it was as good as, if not better than, what you got in restaurants. They would shovel up the noodles with tablespoons after they had put some of Han's Chilli Sauce in it, thumping the end of the bottle with the palm of their hands until their palms became red and thick drops of the sauce, pale green, like something that flows in drains, had fallen out sluggishly. She had started making these steaming diversions – noodles and soups – playfully about ten years ago. And now she dialled the number of Mohit's house. It was picked up by Mohit's cousin, Sameer, who was three years younger than him.

'Hello!' he said, hoarse and loud. He sounded urgent and ready, as if he had been shouting all this time at the top of his voice.

'Hello,' said Bhaskar's mother.

The female voice took Sameer aback. A note of wonder came to his voice.

'Yes?' he said softly (though he found it difficult to speak softly).

'Can I speak to Mohit?'

There was a stunned silence. Then Sameer found his voice; he shouted at his normal volume – 'Ei, Mohit' and

Mohit's voice in the background, slightly superior, and heavy after it had recently broken, wanted peevishly to know, 'What is it?' Sameer was like the boy who cried 'wolf' at every opportunity, and no one took his shouts seriously any more. But this time Sameer sounded vindicated, for he had important news: 'It's a girl, she wants to talk to you.' There was silence again. Then, tense and prepared, Mohit's voice came on the phone; and it was easy to visualize Sameer's wide eyes, open mouth, and pricked-up ears behind it.

'Yes!'

'Can you recognize me?'

'Are you sure,' said Mohit in his knowledgeable way, 'that you have the right number?'

'So you don't recognize me.'

'Is this a joke?' asked Mohit stiffly.

'I'm Didimoni.'

There was an embarrassed sigh. Then, complainingly, Mohit cried:

'Didimoni, why didn't you say so to Sameer? This donkey said you were "a girl".' 'Eh Ram!' could be heard from Sameer in the background.

'Never mind that. You two come today for chow mein at my house.'

So that was agreed. They would tell Mohit's mother and all three would arrive together in the evening in an auto-rickshaw.

'How's the pain?' asked Khuku.

'It's a lot less,' said Mini. 'Very little now.'

'You should get a walking-stick, Mini,' said Khuku. 'It'll be much easier for you. Your leg,' and in Bengali the words 'tor pa' sounded so affectionate, as if she were referring to her leg as if it were her daughter, 'won't have to take the weight.'

'No,' said Mini, in her quiet but inflexible way, for she had already made up her mind about this, 'no, Khuku, I can't take a walking-stick everywhere. It's so much trouble getting on to buses. I'll only lose it.'

'Lose it! ... But what of the limp?' said Khuku. Then, 'Anyway, that will go.'

It was so relaxing to have Mini in the house, for it was lonely for Khuku otherwise. But having Mini there made her feel less restless, and not want to go out all the time. It was enough for Khuku to see her sitting on an arm-chair in the hall, reading an old copy of Parashuram or Bonophul whose binding had its threads coming loose; she held the book considerately, which, in spite of its hard cover being out of joint, still had pages that turned like new ones. She had read these stories before, and was re-reading them now, as she always did when she had a free moment, deriving a great, calm pleasure from them

– for no one, looking at the serious expression on her face, would have been able to deduce that these were extremely funny stories. The household continued in its normal way around her; and she sat there in one corner, disturbing no one, in her cotton sari, her feet in sandals, and the book resting in her lap. She had bathed and was ready before lunch, but never reproached anyone if lunch was late. It was not that she and Khuku had a great deal to talk about; but if Khuku wanted to complain about someone, or voice a worry, Mini listened, nodding her head gravely, or bursting into a short laugh, and after Khuku had finished, she would say, 'He shouldn't have said that,' or 'Oh, don't bother about them.' It was as if she understood Khuku perfectly.

They had been best friends since they were children. And, though she had married and had a child of her own, now a young man doing research in economics in California, Khuku had always been, from their first irresponsible schooldays in Sylhet, the childish one. Mini, though a few months younger at sixty-five, and by some curious distant relation a niece, had the older, calmer, more self-contained air; it was as if living alone so many years with her elder sister, teaching geography and Bengali at a school, gave her this centre of self-sufficiency which comforted Khuku. She was a judge's daughter; in Sylhet, Khuku, whose father had died early, and who was the second youngest of seven undisciplined children, used to spend afternoons sucking pickles and chattering on the porch of Mini's house: they were both given to bouts of frivolous laughter. Khuku hated boys; Mini went to sewing class without a needle. And Khuku – Khuku had gone on to become a mother, and Mini had become a schoolteacher – both facts were equally difficult to believe.

41

But Mini had her own shy, repressed side, which rarely came to light. For instance, after the luxury of bathing in Khuku's house, she, in her unsmiling unostentatious way, splashed eau-de-cologne on herself; and she had her preferences in brassières, liking those that had small coloured flowers on their cups. But all this was her own secret, for then she covered herself in a large maternal white blouse and a neutral cotton sari. More than a year ago she had got arthritis, which had worsened till, with a deep breath, she had to prepare herself for her journey every morning to school, walking, step by step, tentatively down the stairs, leaning more upon her good foot, and then limping very slowly, but in a measured, symmetrical way, past the compound, through the gates, into the lane, onto the bus, and alighting finally near the school. The children in the compound had grown used to her new walk, for all things become slow with time, and her body too had almost got used to it. But she told Khuku, 'It cut as if someone were putting salt upon it, Khuku re.' 'There is *no* solution but complete rest,' declared Khuku, saying 'complete rest' in English. 'And do you want to become a cripple?' 'No,' said Mini quietly. Thus had Mini's recuperation and long holiday begun in Khuku's house.

Khuku had her own unworldly routines. She sang, to the accompaniment of her own harmonium, and her voice was still young and as tuneful as it had been when she was sixteen. Her voice was almost a miracle. In Sylhet and Shillong, it had shone, but, for one reason or another, life had passed by without fame coming to it. She could not be bothered. Now when people who lived in that Shillong were reminded of Khuku, they said remotely: 'You mean Khuku Biswas, the one who used to sing?' and they recalled a thin girl in a sari, her hair tied in a plait, standing on a stage before a mike, and outside the narrow steep hills of Shillong winding and winding, and Khasia children with red cheeks and high cheek-bones sitting by the roadside. 'She got married and went to England, didn't she?' And here she was again, still sitting before the harmonium, still conscientious about her vocal exercises, though she had tired a little of the delicate beauty of Tagore songs and sang Nazrul and Atulprasad these days. Sometimes, indeed, contrarily, it seemed to her that Nazrul Islam was greater than Tagore, and she had begun to sing again a Hindu devotional kirtan which this Muslim poet had composed in a moment of ecstasy, which she had learnt as a child of seven:

> *How could I be happy at home?*
> *For if my Shyam has become a yogi*
> *Then as a yogini with him I'll roam.*

Her husband loved this song; he sat listening to it very solemnly, as if he had a hot potato in his mouth.
Then:

> *But if it's earth he wants*
> *Then I'll be the earth at his bright feet*
> *For the love of my beloved.*

Always the song returned to its first three lines, where lay its home and heart, its original question and its answer:

> *Aami ki shukhe lo grihe rabo?*
> *Aamar Shyam jodi ogo jogi holo shokhi*
> *Aamio jogini hobo.*

Twice a week, Suleiman Hussein came to play the tabla with Khuku. He was something of a dandy; he had a trimmed white beard which he dyed black before major musical performances. A slim man with a small paunch, he wore a different kurta with his white churidars whenever he could, and a black Kashmiri sleeveless jacket in the winter; he was irritating – but punctual. 'Didi!' he would cry out at four o'clock, whether Khuku was sleeping or not, 'Didi, don't you want to start?' 'So you've arrived exactly on time again – like Yama, the god of death.' Suleiman would blink. Then he would begin to cackle with laughter, the sides of his eyes crinkling and his cheeks swelling and flushing. 'Yama! Didi – Yama! He Ram, he Ram!' Khuku grew impatient when Suleiman laughed at her jokes; she waited equanimously for him to finish. Then a place in the hall was cleared for them by Jochna, and Suleiman yawned, stretched his arms, and began to tune the tabla on the right with a hammer. And Mini watched owlishly from an arm-chair, waiting for Khuku to begin.

THE HOUSE, if it could be called such, was a small stone structure with an asbestos roof.

They were standing before it, one or two of them leaning against the wall that was mapped with a few discoloured patches where the paint had come off; on a tin plate above the door was painted a hammer and sickle in orange, and the letters and numbers: C.P.I.(M.) UNIT 69. Sumanta Saha, a huge lumbering man, had disappeared to the side of the house to urinate into the gutter. Matches were struck against the sides of match-boxes, they rasped, a smell of sulphur sprang into the air, and, patiently, filterless Charminar cigarettes were lit, and their ends dimmed and began to burn. Bhaskar inhaled deeply, contemplated the distance, then exhaled a stream of smoke slowly from his nostrils. He still found a boyish pleasure in smoking – it was something he had discovered twelve years ago with another group of friends – it made him feel solitary, asocial, alone, in communion with the smoke entering and leaving him, but it was not something he did before his parents or relatives. 'Ei – ei, Bhaskar,' said Arun Nashkar, a barely audible whine in his voice. 'Ei – do you have one?' Bhaskar stirred unhappily. 'Dhur,' he said. 'You never bring your own.' 'I'm trying to stop,' said Arun Nashkar sagely. The other's hand vanished into

45

a trouser pocket, retrieving something therefrom, a crumpled golden-coloured cigarette packet which he held out to Arun Nashkar. 'What for?' he asked. But Arun Nashkar did not answer, for he now had a cigarette in his mouth, and Bhaskar had handed him, with the tired air of one who is under a compulsion, his own cigarette to light his with; the cigarettes kissed for a long moment, Arun Nashkar's eyes narrowed and his cheeks hollowed, and then reluctantly, heavily, they parted, Bhaskar took back his and returned it to his mouth, Arun Nashkar breathed and a mist of smoke partially hid his face.

The day was warm, and yet they felt insulated in their slip-overs. Many of them had congregated on the pavement to absorb the sunlight, their hands cupped around bhaads of tea. The meeting was over; Samaresh Hajra had made a speech about the International Monetary Fund, beginning, 'Friends … comrades … our country has opened its doors to the imperialists again …' But now that the meeting was over the room was empty and the doors ajar. When they had come into the room, they had opened the windows on either side, easing down the locks at the top that squeaked when they were moved. Now the dung-smoke that had entered the room during the meeting hung quietly in it. Mosquitoes that had drifted in during the talk still wandered about, searching a human smell. On the young Party members' arms they had left tiny red pustulations; all through the talk there had been the sound of agitated slapping. And, in the poster, Lenin's eyes, above his neat beard and below the dome of his bald head, shone humorously. Here, in the deep green humid Gangetic delta in Bengal, among jack-fruit trees, malaria, and bluebottle flies, was one of the last Socialist governments in the world, and here, in a lane ten minutes away from Ishwar Chandra Vidyasagar Road, was one of its local outposts. 'Ours is an economy of small businesses, small enterprises,' Samaresh Hajra had said. Dramatically, he had taken a fountain-pen out of his pocket. 'This pen is made in our country, India. It may not write as well as a Parker, it may not write at all after a few days' – there was laughter – 'but we have made it ourselves.' What Samaresh Hajra had told them was true – that foreign investment was dangerous to India, though the bourgeoisie, whose needs had made India bankrupt in the first place, were looking forward to it. Then a head had peered in through the door. 'Dada, should I bring tea?' It was the Bihari boy who worked in the tea-shop on the opposite side of the road. During the summer he wore only khaki shorts, and his brown skin shone, but now his head with its crop of dry hair stuck out from a shawl which hung down loosely from his shoulders. The meeting had ended five minutes later. They had trooped out through the door, onto the pavement, cigarettes had been lit, and Narayan, who had shot off, returned, still running, with bhaads of steaming tea on a tray.

Dipen Mandal was a singer and the youngest of that group. He wouldn't have been more than twenty-one years old, and still had no moustache or beard. His mother had died when he was a child, and he had been brought up by his father and aunt; he loved new clothes, and today he was wearing a white shirt with broad collars and light blue trousers with narrow flares. He was just a boy, really, and couldn't keep his eyes off the two sisters in saris who stood on the balcony of the house on the other side of the road. His father, who always wore clean, starched dhutis and kurtas, was a singer too, but perhaps better known as a revolutionary poet who had published two volumes of verse in his youth; both father and son had been present in that long, winding procession pledging support to Cuba and Castro that had gone down from Tollygunge to BBD Baag in September. Dipen was the only one among this group who didn't like tea and didn't smoke because of his voice. He was serious about his singing; he took lessons in classical music from a guru; he practised in the mornings. Sometimes it seemed that he was more interested in singing revolutionary songs than in Party work, but the others in the group were indulgent towards him and treated him like a younger brother and called him Deepu. Standing on the pavement, keeping at an arm's length from the rest, he was humming a vocal exercise, 'Sa re ga, re ga ma, ga ma pa...' Deeply engrossed, peacock-proud, he uttered the first line of a patriotic song: 'O unlock this, unlock this, unlock this door of darkness!'

What happy times they had together! There were dress rehearsals, processions, demonstrations, street-plays, adult education for the illiterate, Dipen Mandal breaking into 'Sing Cominternational' on May Day to the accompaniment of his single-reed harmonium. They had all grown up on the border that separated middle-classness from a fathomless darkness, on the border where a street of middle-class houses ran out to the railway lines and the makeshift huts beyond, the fathomless cricket- and firefly-haunted darkness in which paraffin lanterns were lit; all their lives they had barely managed not to slip off from their haven of school-books and exams. Samaresh Hajra had a younger sister, two brothers in school, and his mother was a widow; for the last two months he had had no job. He was the one who had spoken today of the International Monetary Fund. Only Bhaskar, perhaps, among them, could be said to have come from a family that was properly middle class; thus, there was an ineffable aura about his ordinariness – he was held in respect.

There was an old bicycle shop across the road, with mournful floppy tyres hanging like festoons at the entrance. Further on, the road bifurcated, and at that point there was a triangular island of green barricaded by iron railings, some of them missing, in which there was a bust of Swami Vivekananda, painted white. What eyes Vivekananda had – eyes of deep unwavering calm which remained untroubled by the insistent hooting of the state transport buses going past. The grass that grew around the bust had become coarse and dry, and seemed more so in the winter. Cows, spent, unworldly, idol-like, sometimes reclined before that statue. Girls and boys knelt enquiringly on the pavement, searching endlessly for souvenirs, emitting urgent cries in the dusk, snot dried around their noses. At five o'clock in January it would become dark, and the small lights glowing in windows would serve as a human counterpoint to the sunlight that scattered and spread at the turning of the road. In the tea-shop, shawls would cover the tops of the timid and cold-fearing Narayan's and Narayan's uncle's heads, two Bihari expatriates, while tea continued to brew and swirl in the blackened kettle. But now it was bright, and Sumanta Saha, who had finished his bhaad of tea, threw it on the pavement and crushed it underfoot like an egg-shell.

'Bhaskar!' he called to the one who was still unsmilingly smoking. 'Are we meeting on Friday, then?'

Bhaskar was in a dark recalcitrant mood, possessed by the kind of lethargy that people usually succumb to in the summer, or just before the monsoons, in June. He lifted his large black long-lashed eyes.

'Hu.'

'Have you xeroxed the script for the play?' asked the large Sumanta in his thin childlike voice.

He was speaking of the street-play they were to perform in Behala, an allegorical tale about life in capitalist Russia, called *The Fall of Ashoke*, written by the talented young man whose mind engendered almost all their plays, Arjun Dastidar.

'Yes,' said Bhaskar, opening his mouth a little.

'Then I'll see you on Friday,' said the big man, reassured. 'I'm going home now – you know why. I forgot to bring money with me – just pay my twenty-five paisa to Narayan, Bhaskar, I'll give it to you on Friday.'

'There's no need,' said Bhaskar.

That night, after Haridasi, wordlessly and systematically, had beaten the mattresses with a jhata, and laid out the soft damp white quilts on the bed, and lit the Tortoise mosquito coils in the rooms, while Bhaskar and Piyu watched the English film on television downstairs, Bhaskar's father turned the knobs for the medium and short wave on the radio – to listen to who knows what – producing a curious but characteristic mélange of noises, strange haunting voices that would be interrupted by fading frequencies, desperate snatches of the Oriya and Assamese news, the spiritual monotonous far-away sound of a raag being sung, then being swallowed up by a whistling, humming vacuum, strains of Greek music, the nasal lisping of Arab voices: it was after eleven, and India seemed to come alive on the air-waves in ghostly manifestations, and beyond it, the world. And it was an old habit of his, going back to the first months of his marriage, to stand thus at this hour turning the knobs, allowing his soul to plunge into the vast uncharted territory that the radio so mysteriously tuned into at night. He had missed the news on television, and the English, Bengali, and Hindi news on the radio; now he was hoping that some mysterious nocturnal station would tell him what the new Indian cricket team was. 'Foolish to have left Gower out,' he told himself.

'We should go somewhere on a trip,' said Bhaskar's mother slowly, lying on the bed. 'Maybe Darjeeling.'

'At this time of the year?' said her husband. 'No! Do you know how cold it will be there now?'

'Somewhere, then. Somewhere in the South.'

She lay there, thinking. She went on pilgrimages with her sister or with Piyu to Gopalpur, or to Nabadweep where Chaitanya had preached; they all went for picnics in the winter with oranges and flasks of tea to Diamond Harbour or Digha; and, once, over the last three years, with Mohit and Puti and others they had taken a plane – a great event – to Kathmandu, and once to the hills of Kalimpong. They had gone during the Pujas, in September, when it was hot and humid and the insects named after the goddess herself – Shyama – sought out the light bulbs and lay dead on the floor in the morning. It gave them great pleasure, in that heat, to pack up jackets and cardigans and caps, and return a week later with photographs in colour with themselves – recognizably themselves, but subtly changed as if by a magic spell – standing against a blue and green back-drop of hills, embarrassed or jubilant smiles on their faces, Bhaskar slouching, Piyu sullen and self-conscious, Puti glorious and histrionic, and a little frown always, always residing between Bhaskar's father's eyebrows, all of them having donned those woollen caps and cardigans. There, among those misty hills, waking to early sunrises, they made friends with other Bengalis like themselves, who too were visiting from Calcutta, and whose names they forgot once they had returned to the city. Perhaps Bhaskar's mother loved these excursions more than anyone else. For three-quarters of her life, she had never been able to leave this house and go anywhere, except for those brief pilgrimages to Gopalpur and Nabadweep. But now she wanted to go to Haridwar and Kashi on the banks of the Ganga, to the long swinging bridge in Lakshmanjhula, all the sacred places she had heard of, hidden in mountains or in repose by rivers; she wanted to go south to Kerala, and to Cochin, and Kovalam, and Kanyakumari, the tip of India. Perhaps even to Manik, across the seas ... She had a black spot on the sole of her right foot – she had had it since childhood – which meant that she would travel widely. She had always treated it as a kind of joke, but lately, without her realizing it, it seemed to have released its powers, and her feet were planting themselves on strange grounds she had never thought of visiting.

Her husband loved this city. He loved its fish, rui and katla and koi with black oily scales, and during the monsoons he would cry out a truism that he repeated with great ardour at this time every year: 'Ilish is the king of fishes!' He was a tense man, it was difficult to discuss anything with him without getting into a serious argument – all his life he had been like that. But take him out of Calcutta, and one could imagine him becoming unhappy and quiet. Thirty years ago, he had come to this city and got married. Since then, its air had changed, till now a nimbus of smoke and dust and fumes surrounded it always. But he loved it as one who had come here and made his life here. Here he had launched his small business, here he had had his children, Bhaskar, Manik, and Piyu; they had gone to the same school and read Bengali and English and read the same subjects, and in them, in the way they spoke and in what they spoke of, he saw Calcutta more truly than in himself; they were the children of this city. As they grew up, from dark helpless bundles to two thin boys who loved cricket and feared insects, and a tongue-tied girl who made orange squash by herself with a spoon and a tumbler, to the three different beings they were now, he seemed to have seen them changing as rapidly and miraculously as if he had been witnessing a plant growing over a month, and as they grew a sense of loss came to him, a sense of distance from the Bhaskar and Piyu and Manik that twenty years ago he had dreamed vividly they would be, though he was not sure what the dream was. But three children had become ghosts as three children had grown up, and only he, it seemed, had remained the same. Who was he? Time and Calcutta seemed to pass through him like water. He had come here and fallen in love with Gariahat, its fish and vegetable market with its shouting community of vendors and darting basket-boys. That was Calcutta. Then, in 1971, not far away, Bangladesh was created, and the refugees who had come to the city set up their small stalls in Gariahat. It was his life; no one else would know it.

KHUKU AND Mini sat side by side on two arm-chairs in the hall, facing the veranda.

Each day, at some point, they talked of the Muslims. They talked of how, by the next century, there would be more Muslims than Hindus in the country. Mini, being the teacher, had the facts and figures. She told Khuku that 'population control' was meant for Hindus alone, and Khuku, listening to Mini, began to see Muslims everywhere. They grew excited about the azaan on the loud-speakers, and about Muslim festivals in which people beat themselves with whips and cords. Once, when talking thus, and saying, 'They should change as well, not just the Hindus,' they had forgotten that Abdullah the tailor, who had come to take measurements, was sitting, only a small distance away, self-consciously on the sofa, more self-conscious about sitting on the sofa than about anything the two might have said. Khuku had bit her tongue and indicated Abdullah with her eyes to Mini, and said quietly, 'He didn't hear us,' and then, 'Even if he did, so what?'

They were both in old age, though they did not feel it. Khuku's face had a few noticeable wrinkles; and these only appeared, emphasized, when she had not slept for two nights. Her grey hairs were camouflaged by the black, and the obvious ones 'touched up' with mehndi or dye. There were days when she wandered around the house with mehndi in her hair, which smelled like mud or manure till she had washed it off. And her small body, loved in its present incarnation by her husband and child, had remained constant over the last twenty years. And Mini's even smaller body, dark skinned, the forehead glowing with the hair pulled back in a small bun, the eyes upon the face not large but frank, as Khuku remembered them from girlhood, now hidden by spectacles —she was the same Mini. The only difference between them were the marks on Khuku's belly from the Caesarean operation, for she had once borne a child, while Mini's belly, bulging with a natural plumpness, was smooth and untouched.

'BJP,' said Khuku, her eyes larger than usual. 'I might even vote for the BJP. Why not?'

They spoke defiantly and conspiratorially, as if they were playing a prohibited game. They would stop once Shib arrived at the house.

'In fact, it was no bad thing that they toppled that mosque,' said Mini. She looked small and powerful, as if she had unsuspected energies within, and could have gone up to the mosque and toppled it herself, alone. She had quite forgotten about the pain in her leg.

'No bad thing,' said Khuku, who agreed with everything that Mini said.

But Khuku and Mini did not believe in Ram or Krishna; Khuku's personal deity, which she might have created herself, or which had possibly been created by her mother, was one she called Bipad Nashini, or Destroyer of Distress, whom she saw as a maternal figure who watched over her and her family, and whose name she muttered whenever she was worried: 'Hé bipad nashini, hé bipad nashini.' This mysterious female divinity resided, it seemed, in Khuku's heart, there she had her home in the world, and from there she sprang to life when her name was uttered in that worried, childlike way by Khuku.

Long before she either disbelieved or believed in things, Khuku had heard of the Muslims, or the Musholmaan, as a child. Her world was then populated by her mother, her brothers, and by a huge family of ghosts and spirits. It became dark soon, there was no electricity, and she could scarcely keep her eyes open; in the next room, her elder brothers and elder sister and mother kept on talking. In that world, her closest companions were her younger brother, Bhola, who was then no more than an idiot who had barely learnt to speak, and Pulu, who was older than her by a year. Pulu believed in the next life, and in other worlds, where daylight was a soft purple, and he was always getting cuffed on the head by his elder sister for asking so many questions and being such a nuisance. He was brilliant at arithmetic and a great crammer and knew all the tables by heart. Khuku loved him very much, and one of the first words she had ever spoken, 'Dada,' referred to him. It was he who first told her of the Hindoos, who were a fierce wandering tribe with swords who cut up everything in their path, as their very name, 'Hin-doo', suggested, and Musholmaans, he explained, were ghosts who haunted the dark and hilly regions of Sylhet.

IN THE afternoon, Bhaskar reclined on the bed; his back
had been troubling him again. He had not made the
long journey to the factory because of it; instead, he had
had a full meal, and now he sought the most appropriate
position for his head on the pillow. In the morning, he
had woken up with limbs quite frozen, and had had to ask
his mother for help to get off the bed; he had hopped
about like a huge injured bird. Now he lay back and
sighed, with a book on yoga in one hand. The pages were
light and wispy, and the paper was peppered and flecked
with impurities; the Bengali print was faded. Almost each
page had another page with a photograph facing it, smoky
black and white photographs that were really blue-grey,
with figures in them doing various asanas, the first two
pages of photos being occupied by Surjomukhi Maharaj,
who had written the text, a fat, fair, bearded holy man
with small eyes and a smile on his face. The rest of the
photos were of thin unnamed men in brief white jangias,
immortalized in that blue and white world in dozens of
strange postures, straining, as it were, to become something else, to fly, to be transmogrified. The text made
unexpected revelations in a deadpan way: '*Muktabayu-
asana*: This is good for the digestion. Those who do this
daily will not suffer from gas or stomach problems. First

lie on your back and breathe in, then slowly raise both your knees...' Bhaskar must have read the book more than twenty times, for he had bought it from the Dakkhinee bookshop when he was fifteen. He could only just remember the shopkeeper taking it out of the window, slapping the powdery dust off it, and handing it to him. Bhaskar had at that time been passing through a long phase of interest in yogis and Mr Universes, an interest he had passed on to Manik as well, and their hero and idea of perfection had then been Monohar Aich, the great Bengali body-builder, who had muscles swelling and hardening on every part of his body. Since he had acquired the book, Bhaskar had been much stirred by the importance of the names of the exercises – padmasana, virasana, muktasana – and had interred them as a kind of knowledge. In those days, his mother was always asking him, 'Have you done your schoolwork?' and a great lethargy and reluctance filled him as he dragged himself to his textbooks. But, whenever he could, he read the articles in *Sportsweek* and *Sportsworld* about Shyam Thapa or Pelé, or flicked through the pages of the yoga book till he had become familiar with the descriptions of the asanas and those thin, bare-chested men in their state of arrested transport, with the pale luminous white wall behind them. When their mother looked at Bhaskar and Manik, she saw two wiry, restive boys, but she also saw, in their eyes, in the way they walked, in the way they spoke occasionally, what they saw themselves as – Tarzan and Hercules – and, vividly, she could see them increasing and filling out to their imaginary proportions, to their ideal, while, at the same time, being able to see them for the two thin boys they were.

Bhaskar had never been, although he was a great

shirker of studies, and also a great day-dreamer, a particularly rebellious boy. If his feet ever accidentally brushed against a book, for instance, he immediately and swiftly touched his forehead and chest with his index finger in quick, absent-minded repentance, and as, in those days, books and magazines that were being read by Bhaskar, Manik, or their mother would always be lying by pillows or on the middle of the bed, because the bed served as floor and bed and table at once, and because Bhaskar's normal mode of locomotion in the room was quick skips, jumps, and runs from bed to floor and floor to bed, his feet were always grazing books, and he, at least five or six times a day, was engaged in making that brief, absent-minded gesture. His day-dreams were the usual ones dreamt by Bengali boys of his age: of alternative lives that were much like the lives of Swami Vivekananda and Subhas Chandra Bose. At the age of seven, he had been given a thin book with broad, flapping pages called *We Are Bengalis*, with small biographical tales about Vivekananda and Vidyasagar and Tagore, each prefaced by a portrait of a serene and grave face; and some of the stories fired him with pride, and others made him cry. Once he understood what a wonderful thing it was to be a Bengali, and that he was Bengali himself, he went around the house chanting, 'We are Bengalis! We are Bengalis!' and this echo, predictably, was taken up by Manik, who had no inkling of what it meant.

He had read the book on afternoons much like this one many years ago, lying on his stomach and flicking the pages. The story he liked the best was the one about Swami Vivekananda, who was once an ordinary man called Narendranath Dutta. Narendranath wanted a simple answer to a question he had asked men of several religions

– Buddhism, Christianity, Islam, Hinduism – and the question was: have you seen God? Only Ramakrishna said, 'Yes: yes, I have seen Ma Kali!' Testing Ramakrishna, Narendranath placed a picture of Kali under his mattress, and the saint leapt up in agony as if he had been burnt. Ramakrishna, seeing Narendranath was a great disciple, gave him the name Vivekananda, and Vivekananda, journeying to America, homeless in Chicago, and then put up by a kindly old lady, brought glory to India by addressing the Parliament of World Religions with his speech: 'Brothers and sisters of America...' For a long time after, Bhaskar remembered every detail of this story, and he seemed to be there with Vivekananda when he was Narendranath and wandering from temple to church, and he entered the strange world where, with Narendranath, he met Ramakrishna, and he was there with Ramakrishna as well, when he sat in a trance and saw Kali before him, appearing little by little, her blue skin, the pink of her tongue, the black of her hair, and then becoming whole, and he came back to the real world with a little of the smoke and incense and terror still upon him. Through those days, as he walked from one room to the other in the afternoon, or came out from the toilet, he wondered if it was possible to see Saraswati or Durga or any divinity by chance, for a minute, for no reason. Then, one day, he asked an older, fifteen-year-old cousin who lived in North Calcutta, 'What would happen if you saw a god? Is it possible?' 'A god?' said the cousin. 'Yes, like Kali or Durga. Does it ever happen?' The cousin's face became suddenly sad. 'Yes it does,' he said. 'But those who see a god invariably die.'

In Bhaskar's mother's handbag lay two photographs in a white envelope. There they lay, removed from the sunlight, unless they were taken out and subjected to curious scrutiny. One was a girl from Jodhpur Park, twenty-four years old, in a printed sari, with a small smile on her face, her body in profile, and the other was in black and white, from Dum Dum, with studio lighting falling on her hair. Although her features were not perfect, it was the first girl for whom Bhaskar's mother had a slight preference, and had let enter into her heart a tiny emotion, a small attachment, though it could not really be called emotion or attachment for these are things you feel for people you know. Perhaps it was because her face had a patience and tolerance, and her personality a seriousness that was emphasized, rather than diminished, by that small smile, the gaily printed sari denoting a kind of openness – but these were things she said to no one, not even to herself. The photographs were really for Bhaskar to look at, though he never did so properly, but glanced at them for a moment and put them away, as if they hurt his eyes. Then they had been carefully and judiciously considered by Piyu, and laughingly and embarrassedly gazed at by Bhaskar's father, and very seriously, and not without excitement, looked at by Puti, and now they lay in the handbag again, two ordinary objects that had unexpectedly entered their lives, two paper-thin cards, called photographs, with human faces upon them.

Meanwhile, Bhaskar went each day to the factory; at other times attended his Party meetings; but most enjoyed the numerous rehearsals in the evenings for plays that would be performed on streets and even in theatres. These one- or two-act compositions possessed solemn messages, each one a parable or political allegory set in

medieval India, or in an unnamed land that was sufficiently fantastic, sufficiently unreal, the citizens of this
twilit world enacting events that had taken place only
recently – the assassination of Rajiv Gandhi, the frag-
menting of the Soviet Union, and, lately, the violence
done to Muslims by Hindus. These disparate images, that
had colluded somehow in Arjun Dastidar's head, were
made material and brought alive in a small room with
white walls in Tollygunge, with a 100-watt bulb shining
from the ceiling. Like inquisitive and loyal visitors, the
sound of trams clattering back and forth outside and the
spun pink-white winter smoke surrounded the players in
the room and listened to their every word and every
recapitulation and revision. Tender, destitute noises, of a
cat meowing, and maidservants chattering and laughing
as they walked by, transfigured what was beyond the wall.
To Bhaskar, as he tried on a costume, or cried out in
literary Bengali, 'Alas! What was my mistake?' (for their
plays were full of aggrieved shouts and excited excla-
mations), there came back his childhood world of intrigue
and assassinations, courage and injustice, and so, utterly
convinced, he clutched his breast with his hand and fell.
For what was creation but a great theatre, with swarga,
with its deities in every mansion, and blue akaash, born
of God's breath, and pataal, the deep, dark, crouching
abyss below, perpetually exhaling spumes of dark smoke
and protesting with many voices, and, in between, man, a
tiny, wonderful, living creature, travelling in his frail craft,
facing, astonished but fearless, the endless, dramatic vicis-
situdes of pataal and swarga? Who would remember him?
Blood-curdling cries emanated from the room, followed
by laughter.

Confused moths wandered in from outside and settled,

becoming invisible until you saw them, a small triangular patch on the wall. When they were disturbed for some inexplicable reason, they burst into life and floated hither and thither, casting shadows much larger than themselves. The wall was always full of the shadows of faces, of bodies, of the slope of shoulders, the liquid outlines of loose clothes, of shawls, of pyjamas, a play of pictures accompanying messages conveyed from one kingdom to another, and cunning murders being committed. And who were these shadows but Bhaskar, Samaresh, Sumanta, Nikhil, Dipen, robbed of their features and invested with a curious darkness and poignance, shadows where the bright white lime-painted wall became mysteriously blue? And the moths, when one noticed them, reminded one of the alleyways, of green shuttered windows with iron grilles behind them, and the perpetuity of habitation, where they lived with children, young men, fathers, mothers, resting on a wall next to a calendar with a picture of Shiv or Durga, or behind cupboards with piles of old shirts and saris, or distracting two boys as they sat down to study at their table. Such tranquillity they possessed – not a wall existed in Calcutta that would not give them repose!

And now a link was sought to be made between one person and another, between Bhaskar and a girl, who had been growing up all the while in this city, secretly, while Bhaskar had been wearing half-pants, and buying *Sportsweek* and reading Mandrake comics, and going to Gariahat Market with Robida to buy a water bottle, and riding on trams, his shirt clinging to his back with sweat – someone, somewhere else, was growing up as well, in as random and unpredictable a way, in a little self-absorbed world of day-to-day desire. There were so many places it could have happened – in Mandeville Gardens, in one of the lanes that surrounded the South Point School; in a nook in Jadavpur; in the half-countryside, half-urban settlement of Tollygunge; in Jodhpur Park, past Dhakuria Bridge, by the daily swell of smoke and traffic. There she had grown up, dragging her feet in chappals, wandering indolently in the veranda, making friends with girls called Bapsi and Mintu. Now it was study time, and now it was evening, with the tube-light switched on, and, all through her growing up, the city, like a great arm, had protected her, and kept her hidden and nameless.

TWICE A WEEK, they'd go to a nursing home in Dhakuria. It was a new place, built on a field that had once been empty. A by-lane of two-storeyed houses and trees led to it. Because the building itself was new, with a flat white façade that had red borders, it looked like a mirage, as all new things do in Calcutta. And then it had those tinted glass doors at the entrance that kept its interior a secret and imaged the world outside, and those new, flourishing money-plants on the porch that shone so, that they seemed to be made of plastic. Not to speak of the watchman in khaki, like a large ragged doll, the winter light falling on the stubble on his face.

'Ma Sharada Devi nursing home,' said Khuku to Mritunjoy, the driver.

The words were enough to please Mini. She was something of a devotee of Ramakrishna and Swami Vivekananda; had long been one; not a formal one, but one who'd read their books, life stories, and sayings.

'Who built the nursing home, re?' asked Mini.

'I don't know,' said Khuku, who'd never had much interest in facts. She relied on instinct. 'It's a good, clean place,' she said.

Some doctor had recommended it to her when she'd needed a check-up (both check-ups and age had nudged

Khuku, who felt so inwardly young, and surprised her into disbelief), and she had recommended it to Mini when she realized she required treatment. In her mind, the place had become associated with healing and a certain stage in her and Mini's life, and afternoons when her husband was at work.

Her husband at work – seventy years old, hair half grey; yet the five thousand rupees coming in per month from a 'sick' company was useful in all kinds of small ways. It needn't *remain* sick, now that her husband was in it. But lately Shib had said, sombre in his sleeveless slip-over, 'I don't know why they've taken me.' He'd shaken his head. 'The government isn't interested in putting money into the company. I don't know if they expect me to perform some miracle and put it on the right course again.' He was unlikely to make any miracles happen, presiding over in his active old age this company he'd known since childhood. 'I've heard that there are some people who resent that money's being diverted from a loss-making firm to pay my salary – so it's best not have any expectations.'

Here, at the entrance of the lane, was a sprawling rubbish-heap of an unimaginable colour – but the two women in the car wouldn't notice it. Mini was wearing a white tangail sari with a slender green border, and a dark cardigan; bent forward slightly, she was a mixture of light and dark this afternoon. Many times Khuku had per-suaded her to wear brighter colours, but she had always refused; not saying why, but on the unspoken grounds of her age, and being single; it was just a preference and a belief she had.

Through traffic jams, bursts of exhaust fumes, a mad chorus of car horns, they'd come, passing the 'boulevard' in Gariahat, with its tinsel and Christmas caps hanging from the stalls, and its portraits of Ramakrishna and imitation Rembrandts, empty exercise books and jars of spices and generators; then the roundabout at Gol Park. Through all this they'd come.

The nursing home rose before them like a mirage. All the doctors attending to Mini had come to know both of them well – and addressed them as 'mashima'. There was Dr Sarkar and Dr Majumdar, both of them young enough to be Khuku's sons; both most courteous, and attentive to Mini, saying, 'Mashima, sit here,' and, 'Tell me, how is the problem now?' Khuku remembered her son when she saw these two young doctors, and then she told them about him; and they seemed interested and always had five minutes to spare to have a relaxed chat with her. They'd got to know how Bablu was in America, doing a doctorate in economics, and how her husband was still working in a company. 'That's good,' Dr Sarkar had said. 'Men age quickly if they don't work.' Khuku had been pleased with this; she'd thought, Then it doesn't matter that it's not a good company, at least he's doing a job. When they examined Mini, Khuku either sat in one of the chairs in the hall, or stood in the corridor outside which received weak sunshine from the frosted window on the door at its end, the door that opened onto a dusty space at the back where the cars were parked. She thought how strange life was, that she was here and Bablu was in America and her husband in the office, and that there was a clean nursing home in Calcutta with good doctors; she was full of wonder at how one person ended up in one place and someone else in quite another.

When they'd finished they headed back the same way, but going down the by-lane Khuku was always tempted to visit the house, in one of the lanes nearby in Jodhpur Park, her elder sister had lived in. Of course, her elder sister was dead; but her daughter, Puti – Khuku's niece – and Manas, her son, were still there, living in different flats in the same house; as were her grandchildren, Khuku's grand-nephews, Puti's son, Mohit, and Manas's, Sameer. Both were fond of Khuku, their 'Didimoni', but of the two it was the younger, Sameer, less hard-working and mindful of his studies than Mohit, who was the more openly demonstrative of his affection towards his grand-aunt, ready to melt in her arms, and who always had a kiss for her. Puti, too, after the death of her mother, had begun to see Khuku, her only aunt, in another light (although both sisters had been different in every way, including appearance, Puti's mother fair skinned with fine thinning hair, and ten years older than her sister, almost everything about Khuku these days reminded Puti of her mother). She – whom Khuku had called, simply, Didi – had died just over a year ago of Parkinson's disease. Her brain hadn't been affected, thank God; but her movements had been reduced to a minimum until, finally, she hadn't been able to get up from the bed without the help of nurses. At least she hadn't suffered terribly; anyway, it had seemed to Khuku, there was nothing Didi had liked better than lying in bed with a magazine; and this it had been possible for her to do till a few months before she had died; in this sense, it had been a happy ending. When Khuku visited her, she'd find that Didi was still eager to take part in conversations. She'd open her mouth and form a few words to ask a question, and Khuku would have a clear view of her betel-stained upper teeth, which protruded slightly; and when the others gossiped, she'd listen, her eyes moving and registering surprise, disbelief, and amusement. Thank God she had had hired nurses always attending to her – not everyone had a rich son in America to pay for their medical expenses; she might have died much earlier had she not been so well looked after.

Now and then, their voices could be heard; not the voices in which they spoke to Khuku, but those that they reserved for themselves. They did not bother to speak softly; there was no one else in the flat. It had not been so silent since the days of the curfew.

Khuku often thought that three servants were too many to have in the house; there was only herself and Shib; and these three, for large stretches of time in the day, had nothing to do. Then they reigned like angels or demons without another habitation. They were itinerants, of course; three months later, they might not be here. Only Nando, even when he left, returned again and again.

'What do you think you're doing?'

It was Uma. Nando had reached forward and transferred an egg from his plate to hers. The egg was more than an olive branch; it was a testimony of his intentions towards her. Love, or something like it, had possessed him.

Uma had stopped eating; her right arm was poised in mid air.

'What do you think you are doing?' she asked again. 'You're lucky I'm not going to throw the egg into that corner' – she gestured with her head – 'because I don't want to dirty the kitchen and upset mashima. But I'll tell mashima about you.'

Nando stared at his plate. Of late their quarrels always came to these exchanges. Nando was allowed an extra egg daily by Khuku, not because of favouritism but because not long ago he'd been suffering from tuberculosis. He'd contracted it during a spell of unemployment – after being sacked by Khuku – which he'd spent at home, in a basti near Tollygunge, before a reconciliation brought him back to the job.

———

During the curfew a month ago, all had been disorder and silence. Jochna, who was becoming increasingly pretty, had not been able to come to work for two days; there had been tension in her area and fear of violence. It was at such times that the sketchy unfencedness of their existence became palpable, that they must lead lives pereptually and nakedly open to duress. The Muslims had taken out a procession; at night, when usually an owl – Lakshmi's ancient companion and carrier – hooted near the railway crossing, with a tremulous sense of something about to happen, Jochna and her family and other Hindus in the basti had been moved to a nearby Christian school, while the furious Muslims apparently congregated and went about shouting and protesting. So Jochna did not come to work for two days. Ordinarily this would have irritated Khuku, but this time the atmosphere, distant but palpable, of strife precluded any response, unfortunately, except sympathy.

NANDO HAD spent most of his life in Calcutta; he had started out when he was a young man as an assistant to a cook in a sweet-shop. He could not read a single word in any alphabet. In his own home, this small swaggering man would behave like a patriarch and a pest, something between a monarch and hapless vermin, and was considered a nuisance by his wife and even beaten by his son when he drank. He had a grandson, not much shorter than him, who was his only well-wisher; but being at home wrecked his health. Not long after she had taken him back, Khuku had heard him coughing, and saw him lying about like a sack on the carpet, utterly tired. Dr Mitra, who lived nearby, had come down to take a look at this fatigued specimen, and had advised that a test be done, for TB. Apparently it was still widespread in the bastis and areas these people lived in. 'The only difference is that it's as curable as toothache today,' said Dr Mitra. When Khuku had had his sputum tested, the bacillus had been found in it; but, as good as Dr Mitra's word, he was cured now (that had happened two years ago).

HALF IN her sleep, Bhaskar's mother had been seeing them going up, the collapsible gate opening, shutting, opening, shutting, the voices in Vidyasagar Road coming down the narrow passage-way by the house, and then coalescing and coming up the stairs. She needed her sleep; or else she had migraines. From outside came the sound of the occasional bus or car passing down the road; long deafening horns. But nothing frightened the crows.

The boys went straight up to the second storey, and there began their rehearsals. Bhaskar's mother could hear their voices, far away; she was half dreaming and half listening. Upstairs, they were practising their lines between the bed and cupboards and dressing-table; from time to time, one or two of them wandering to look out at the street and the houses on the opposite side. 'Whose house is that, Bhaskarda?' asked Dipen, clutching a mullion and pushing aside a fragment of a curtain and pointing to the house that the window looked out upon. 'That's the advocate's house,' said Bhaskar. 'The advocate died when I was ten, but we still call it the advocate's house.' 'Bhaskarda! Tell Deepu to shut up so that I can say my lines!' said Dhruba, standing in front of the bed. His 'lines' were really an inarticulate roar. A man called Mahesh in a rather dirty dhuti was sitting on the floor with a dholak on his lap; he'd brought it to beat out a rhythm during the chants. But the sounds they made were always being overpowered by the single-minded, protracted hooting of state transport buses. 'We can use my house for rehearsals,' Bhaskar had offered generously; and this explained their presence here.

'OK, let's repeat the lines!'

'Dhiren, stand in place!'

'Allah-hu-akbar!'

'Allah-hu-akbar!'

And then:

'Let's have a tea break...'

They tried their best to simulate the feeling of performing on the streets, and the atmosphere of the street-play they were preparing for, which was two weeks away. They went over their rudimentary but voluble roles with enthusiasm. They loved the freedom and heat of performing on the streets, of being uncircumscribed by the proscenium, the proximity and palpability of the houses that bordered their performance, their gestures spilling over onto the pulse of the ragged audience, the nearness of the street-sky; and they loved the exaggerated sketchiness of their own rehearsals, the lines never wholly or faithfully committed to memory.

'Haridasi!' sighed Bhaskar's mother downstairs, still lying in bed. 'Haridasi!' When the girl had finally appeared, she said, her voice a decibel lower and deeper after her nap, 'Take them tea upstairs.' As Haridasi was turning to go, she said, 'And listen! Give them some biscuits – those biscuits we bought a few days ago.'

SOMETIMES WHEN Bhaskar's mother heard them rehearsing she thought about Bhaskar worrying for the poor people in the world and she thought just how difficult a place to live in and understand the world was. Look after your own, was her own view.

And she was filled with an apprehension that couldn't be put in words when she heard their voices.

Yet he wasn't going to listen; he must give five hundred rupees of the two thousand he earned to the Party.

Unlike her husband, she had a sharp business sense; but her energies must be devoted to the housekeeping accounts. These she kept with great meticulousness, and zeal, little figures and computations inside a note-book. Meanwhile, it was left to her husband and now her son to preside over the business.

She thought, at times, of the family house in Shyaam-bazaar. During her childhood she had not known what it meant to live anywhere but in a great mansion with many rooms, so prosperous that she had not had any idea of penury.

She had left the house when she'd been eighteen, after getting married, though she kept going back to it for this or that festival. But after her father died she didn't feel the urge to visit it as frequently as she had before; it was as if her ties had been loosened a little; even her ties to the world had been loosened slightly, and, although her ambitions and concerns for her children were still in place, it was almost as if she'd let go.

Even her children did not know if they knew her completely. Now, she rubbed her eyes absently in her half-sleep. It was when Bhaskar and Manik were growing up that her life had passed through its worst phase, with Bhola's business going bankrupt. She had been, then, for the first time, full of fear.

Her innate business sense (which she must have inherited from her father, and which had never been put to use) had made her, recently, create a savings account whose foundations had been laid by a sum left in her father's legacy, and she would not let Bhola tamper or interfere with the savings for the purpose of his business; at first, she had not even told him about it. But mixed up with this hard-headed sensibleness were also shades of spiritualism, of irreducible faiths, and thus, there hung in the big room on the second storey, above the clothes-horse, a picture of Ramakrishna sitting cross-legged, and, next to it, a picture of his wife, Sharada Devi. Lakshmi, Saraswati, Kartik, and Krishna sat in the prayer-room, in some way involved with the destinies in this house. This was one side of her that no one could plumb, where this accessible and ever-smiling woman was most herself, and where also lay, not in a rational way, her hopes and fears for Bhaskar, Manik, Piyu, Bhola and herself, in that order.

There was a loud scraping movement upstairs, furniture being moved, and then the sound of feet running. What was happening?

She herself was a bundle of fears she had never grown out of. Doctors, medicines, TABC injections; all these

76

things she ran from, running literally from the last, climbing up the stairs with the sari pulled round her ankles when the health worker used to come on a visit, chased by her children, laughing and weeping at once; thus she had rarely been vaccinated, but had rarely fallen ill as well. This is what perpetually puzzled her sons; that the prospect of contracting a disease should cause her less fear than the simple pin-prick of an injection. For this was the only time – the visit of the health worker – when they saw her frightened and agitated. Her general good health had been cause for some contentment. But she had sensitive ears, and they ached at times. The imbalances of the menopause caused one side of her face to swell occasionally. Her childhood had been spent in the then-prosperous area of Shyaambazaar in North Calcutta, she the third youngest child of a family of three brothers and four sisters, her father doing a very successful business in cheap detergent soap. Her mother had died when she was six, but it was strange to think that she felt she knew her in a way; her picture now hung next to her father's in the house.

Years had passed, and she was left here, suddenly awake, half listening to the traffic outside.

She was closest to the sister immediately younger than her – Reena – and in an album there was a series of silly photographs taken on that day, one and a half years before she was married, by Chhorda ('Right, stand together, you two!') when they had dressed as men, especially for these photographs to be taken, Reena as a police inspector, wearing a real khaki uniform with a cap and a baton, she just as a civilian, both with ridiculous moustaches etched above their lips, and with serious expressions full of suppressed smiles. They, Abha (which was her name) and Reena, were sixteen and seventeen then, and neither had really known what it was to be either a man or a woman; they had posed on the terrace with the other old buildings in the area behind them. At the age of eighteen she had got married.

Ah, her youth, her youth. Her children would never know it.

Then another life began for her, in another house. She found Bhola full of opinions about what was Art and what was not, and about politics; and, vexed as she was by this man, a secret affection grew for him that was inseparable from the exasperation she felt. Life changed; their children grew up; but he did not change. And in the inconsequentiality of such emotions lay a specialness, that it did not matter to the world or to anyone else what his opinions were, as if there had been, alas, a pact between her and him to see what he was really like. Yet what arguments had to be tactfully averted! She had been a fan of Uttam Kumar, but Bhola, she found, thought he was a 'bad actor' and had a 'stupid face', and these revelations came as a shock and at first she could not possibly understand how anyone could think these things about Uttam Kumar. Nevertheless she tried to understand. Music he took very seriously, more seriously than she had ever seen anyone take something like music before – after all, what was it but music? – and he spoke of tunefulness and bad singing. He spoke of the great singers he'd heard when he was a child. All this to her was an alien idiom; thus she never told him, until many years later, that she had learnt the Hawaiian guitar for two years before her marriage, and could just about play three or four Tagore songs like 'It is your beginning, and my end' and 'Are you only a picture?' on it.

How was one to speak to such a man? And such an impractical man: it was almost as if he'd made whatever he wanted of their lives, and she'd sat back and allowed him to do it. At first they used to have arguments. It took years to just properly understand each other. By that time, one part of life was finished.

———

Upstairs, it was quiet again; and she wondered, for a moment, if everything was all right. But she was reassured that they were at work. Sometimes they were loud as demonstrators on the street, and at other times secretive as thieves. There was no telling when they were excited and when planning something quietly.

'BORDA DOESN'T live far from here, does he?'

Returning from the nursing home three days later, Mini asked this question. It was put forward shyly. For it was like something of a holiday for her, to be in the cool, neat, constricted South; these little trips to and from the nursing home were outings, and even now had the air, for her, of freedom. And each new day with Khuku was a measuring out of time; she, Mini, must go back before long, but to be in this part of the city was to explore a world and witness those who had been changed completely.

'Very near here,' Khuku revealed. 'It's round the corner, isn't it?' she asked Mritunjoy. Not far away was Golf Green and that block of flats.

Mritunjoy mumbled words that sounded like 'Yes, mashima.'

Borda, Khuku's elder brother, had stopped going out since last year. Any visit to the little flat in Golf Green was thus welcome. There were lapses in his memory these days. This had happened after the pneumonia infection, when he'd been on the brink of moving across to the other world, and had just managed, in a nursing home in Mandeville Gardens, almost against his will, to come back. Thus, he might not recognize Mini when she visited him today, though she had visited him in the autumn only a year and a half ago, when he'd been healthy. So this is what it came to, those years in Sylhet. He used to wander about Sylhet town with an umbrella, to protect his complexion; dispensing with his studies, he used to gaze softly at girls, some of whom were Khuku's friends. Khuku suffered as her friends, unaware he was her brother, made satirical comments on his tender appraisal. Then he had got tired of that life, and he'd demanded of his mother when he was twenty-six years old, 'Ma, can I get married now?'

But there were, these days, moments of clarity. For instance, recently, when his daughter Beena had been speaking about Bhaskar with her mother, he'd said, 'What – Bhaskar? He's become a Communist hasn't he?' Then he'd gone into a sort of contemplation.

There was a time when he had a great deal of love for his nephews and nieces; but that was obscured now, absolutely, by a veil of silent but complete obsession with personal health and hygiene. A little over a year ago, his only grandson in Jodhpur Park had died at the age of six of a rare form of cancer; yet at the shraddh ceremony for the child, all Borda could worry about was whether he would be able to have his expected meal at the usual time. At times, now, he sat on his bed ruminating. A visit, no matter who it might be, made his eyes light up with happiness. The words he said were hardly audible, because his voice had become soft. Golf Green surrounded him with its identical verandas.

GOLF GREEN. A maze of houses, predominantly off-white and red, with scattered islands of green, dull façades, one lot of houses hiding from another. One could hardly ever quite remember the way, and Khuku had to rely on the man who had a small makeshift stall for ironing clothes as her landmark.

Very small children and cats sat in the balconies.

They came to the staircase on whose side was imprinted, in the style of graffiti, the letters by which one identified Borda's building.

The two got off from the car. Mini walked towards the staircase.

They had not been expected; Borda's wife, this old, faded woman, in fact, had just begun to prepare lunch.

He had been sitting there, alone, a faded red pullover pulled casually over a woollen vest. He happened to turn his head and was taken by surprise to see his own younger sister standing there and said:

'Khuku?'

The room was narrow. To see the familiar and the living in a moment of inattention is sometimes as extraordinary as seeing the dead; or perhaps that was only true of Borda. He stared at Khuku in astonishment.

At Borda's question, Boudi came out of the kitchen. Borda often spoke nonsense these days and she had to check if he was babbling nonsense again.

Although she was only four years older than Khuku, she looked several years older, partly because Khuku looked much younger than her real age, and partly because Boudi herself had aged prematurely. But the strange thing was that over the last ten years she had remained the same; it was as if she could age no more.

'Khuku, Khuku,' said Borda.

'Look who I've brought with me,' she said tolerantly.

'Who's that – is that Mini?' asked Boudi.

WHEN THEY were going back down Southern Avenue, the trees bare, children playing football and smoke rising at the back, she looked twice at Mini and saw that she was unmindful.

'When do you think it'll end?' asked Mini, her jaw jutting out slightly. For the signs of upheaval were still there, the daily killings, for here was a billboard coming up proclaiming Hindu and Muslim amity.

'You mean...'

'I mean you'll never be able to appease them,' said Mini.

What if one mosque had gone – for hundreds of temples had been destroyed before. She could not understand what the fuss was about.

By the lakes, the trees with outspread branches were bare. A few boys were playing football; further away, someone had lit a fire and a funnel of smoke was rising from it.

Promises, always promises. No sooner had the mosque gone down than the government had promised that it would be built again.

'Who'll rebuild those temples?' she asked.

'That's right,' said Khuku. 'No one talks about them.'

They turned left into Gariahat.

Each day the azaan rose in the morning. Over the alley-ways it rose, and the tram-lines, spreading for a radius of over a mile.

This winter had not been a particularly cold one; it had been diffuse and gentle and chilly rather than crystalline in the mornings.

Meanwhile, the muezzin went on praising the virtues of Allah in syllables that sounded like 'laillallah rasulallah', and Allah was great, Allah was good and glorious.

The government did one thing today and another tomorrow. Today they said they would rebuild the mosque, and the next day they failed to honour the statement.

Some people thought they'd been too tolerant in the past.

Some people thought that the whole conception their country had been based on was flawed; so they must start again. Speeches were expended on the 'idea' of the country and what the meaning of that idea was.

The word 'fundamentalism', travelling everywhere and belonging nowhere: people tried to understand what it meant.

They appealed for the razed site to be left as it was, as a memorial to an event. Let the rubble stand.

In one newspaper, a Muslim writer said, 'The heart of the parrot of Hindu fundamentalism beats in the giant of Muslim fundamentalism. Kill the giant, and you will have killed the parrot.'

At half-past ten, a lemon-coloured Ambassador arrived to pick up Khuku's husband. This was a government car. It waited downstairs as Shib wore his trousers and shoes and wound a tie around his collar.

This lemon-coloured car might thus be considered one of the 'perks' of working at Little's. It had a young long-haired driver at the wheel who talked indefatigably and had grown rather fond of Shib, and who took him to the office each day and brought him back. He was, naturally, one of those who'd lose his job if Little's ever ceased to exist, as there seemed every possibility it might; the driver, however, appeared untouched by this possibility, which was more remote to him than his fantasies. 'What was it like in Bombay, sir?' he'd ask; for he was endlessly curious about Bombay. Last week Shib had been to the Writers' Building, to the third floor, where the department that dealt with 'sick' companies was. The department had a resonant name: Industrial Reconstruction Department. Around it the inexhaustible, murmurous business of governance continued. Under its purview fell a number of companies, although the larger firms which were once impressive but now a liability, prehistoric dinosaurs that were in a museum that was constantly being added to, like Indian Iron and Steel and Bengal Potteries, had been bought over by the Central Government; their lives were governed from Delhi; they were maintained like tamed and exotic pets. Infrequently a sincere effort was made to have them privatized and release them from the imprisonment of an artificial existence into a normal life; but immediately the local trade union resisted the move as a betrayal that might cost employees their jobs. The state government took over smaller companies; it watched and waited; and when a company had ceased performing indefinitely it bought its shares, as it had bought Little's.

Mr Seal of the department had been instrumental in employing Shib, indeed tempting him to employment. 'We'll see if it can be done, sir,' he had said six months ago. He was referring to the task – not always mentioned – of reviving the company. 'If anyone can, you can.' He had wiped his forehead and Shib had sympathized with him inwardly. 'If it can't be done, we'll let it go.' 'How can you just let it go?' said Shib. 'That is what I was coming to,' said Mr Seal. 'Because we don't want to take a "negative attitude" at the outset.'

However, after the meeting last week – if one could call that conversation in the warmth of a late January morning across a stack of files a meeting – it had begun to become clearer to Shib that Seal could not back up his words. Perhaps Seal was beholden to someone else; there was always someone invisible in the background who tied your hands down; at any rate, there was always someone to pass the buck on to; Mr Seal seemed reluctant now, and a commitment could be drawn out of him only with great persuasion. But he would not let Shib go; 'Mr Purakayastha, be patient with us,' he said; it was as if he were waiting for an intervention to set things right.

For now what he had suspected all along became

apparent to Shib, that there had been no change of heart, that the government would rather pay the salaries of the employees of Little's until they ran out of spare money rather than allow the company to stand on its own feet, for which of course funds were necessary. And as for Seal and himself, they were divided by a common language; they spoke reasonably enough with each other, but seemingly without any intention of arriving at an understanding. It was the sort of dialogue he'd never taken part in all his working life.

Later, these meetings depressed him; left him a little tired. He waited outside the Writers' Building for the long-haired driver to spot him and pick him up.

In Little's history, in fact, the history of Calcutta could be seen to have been written. First the company created by the Englishman of the same name eighty-five years ago; then the buying over of the company by an enterprising Bengali businessman of the name of Poddar; then the death of Poddar after Independence; quarrels and disputes between his sons; the company gradually going to seed; the take-over of the company by the state government in 1974; and what it was now, something that had a kind of life and breath, an existence, but not a real one.

SCHOOL HAD begun again, the first troubles were behind them, and, in addition to the faint moustache that had formed on Mohit's upper lip and proclaimed his gradual farewell to childhood, the educational system had thrown further responsibility on his young shoulders, forcing him to study each day for the finals one and a half years away, giving him a seriousness beyond his years. After that, a brief respite, and then the upper matriculation, the Joint Entrance ... Only ten days ago he'd been cycling from house to relative's house in the morning. Now his eyes were a little red, because he'd been studying late into the night the past few days. All that had happened before – the end of the tests, the curfew, the troubles far away in Ayodhya, the visit to Bhaskar's house – seemed vague and dreamlike, and the days now, taken up with work and preparation, seemed like a world of perpetual wakefulness.

He was an only child; as was his cousin Sameer. That was neither an accident nor coincidence. Their parents had planned it this way. No more large untidy families like Bhola's; they would devote all their attention to their one child.

Khuku said to Mini: 'I've never seen anyone who studies quite so hard as Mohit. He wakes up at five in the morning…' She shuddered, because she'd hated studies at school; but Mini, being a schoolteacher, looked impressed.

Puti would converse with Mohit as if he were a grown-up. And in some ways, he was – with his father away on tours he often substituted as the 'man' in the house. And yet he was shorter than he should be at his age, and was any day expected to shoot up.

'Why not?'

'Do I have to answer that? You know that next year is your "final" year.'

The year of the 'final' – it had been waiting for him, it seemed, like a mythical mountain, always there, but coming nearer and nearer; and now it was in sight.

'And time will fly.'

'I couldn't study the way he does,' said Khuku to Mini after a few moments. 'That boy is ambitious and knows how to look after himself. Unlike that other idiot, Sameer…'

Last year his grandmother – Khuku's elder sister – had died. (That had been a few months after Bhaskar, to the bemusement of all, had joined the Party and even Mohit's grandmother had heard and whispered her disbelief.) There had been a sleepless air at home as she had lapsed into a coma, then passed away, then been taken away to the crematorium. It had been something like it was now, with the exams coming up – the confusion of a proper sense of time, the feeling that someone familiar had suddenly gone away, the strange sense that the absence was temporary. It was still strange that his grandmother, who had hardly moved for the last two years of her life, should have left and never returned. Meanwhile, he swotted for his exams and his eyes hurt. A year ago, his mother's eyes had become red with a brief but intense burst of weeping when his grandmother had died, but he had been unable to shed a tear.

But now he was bargaining for something else, something of possible interest; his Bhaskarmama had asked him to come to a rehearsal, probably give them a hand; 'We're busy and we need some help,' he'd said in a way that made Mohit feel an old tenderness towards him, 'and we need to get a message across.' And of course it was a message of great and pressing importance. This feeling of tenderness, which might turn into something more serious, even a commitment, was precisely what his mother wanted to preclude; moreover, there was no time now for anything but studies; secondly, there is no doubt that the young are impressionable at certain moments in their lives, although his mother had every confidence in her son's essential, practicable level-headedness.

Yet this city that Mohit had been born into seemed sometimes like a bad dream to Puti, with posters, and endless peeling political messages on the walls.

He was still awkward with girls. But he would not be here long. Little did he know that two years from now he would be in America. Around him, the city decayed. This boyhood, of private tutorials, practising maths questions from past question papers, of being in the school quiz team (only the other day he'd represented his school, with three others, at Don Bosco), of playing football in the parking lot in the corner, of visiting Bhola dadu's house and eating pittha, none of it would last long. It would give way to a brief adolescence and then he would be gone to America, where his uncle was. Before long he'd sit for his Scholastic Aptitude Test.

Childhoods were terribly brief these days.

OFTEN, WHEN Mini sat late in the afternoon on one corner of the sofa, and she shut her book and looked up, facing the veranda, she would see the sun setting in the right-hand corner. The sky glowed red, as if at the slow aftermath of a conflagration. These, the last days in Khuku's house.

Almost as if she were exploring a house she did not know very well, she got up and began to walk – she came out into the space of the dining-room, and went past the table.

Khuku must be sleeping inside. Any moment she would be out here.

The doctor at the nursing home (what was his name – Sarkar? – he wouldn't be over thirty) had told her, without force, but not without a doctor-like gravity, she should begin to do some exercises immediately ('Just once or twice a day, mashima,' he'd said.) It was a matter of how best to treat this leg, newly healing: it was almost as bewildered, tentative, and over-confident as a child, and she must give it rest but it must learn to walk again as well. She was going nowhere – just turning round the dining-table and returning to where she had started.

The pain was gone; she noticed this. It was almost gone. She was lulled by a vortex of calm, the familiarity and spaciousness of Khuku's flat. And yet this flat, full of pretty things and tinkling curios, was both a second home and a cave of wonder to her, so unlike any other place in Calcutta, so that sometimes it seemed to her she'd suddenly woken up to it, to a brief sojourn, had been borne here in her sleep without being conscious of the journey.

She continued walking, as the sun ebbed outside.

———————

Mini had suddenly come to Khuku's mind last month, in December; like a sudden pressure on Khuku's conscience; a few days, as it happened, after the troubles in Ayodhya. Mini had explained to her on the phone that she hadn't been able to go to school for two days because of the pain from her arthritis.

And she'd temporarily become preoccupied with the idea of bringing her to her house; till in a few days she succumbed to the pull that her friend was exerting on her unconsciously.

'Let me bring Mini here,' Khuku had said to Shib. 'And then I can look for a doctor. I think the main problem is that she doesn't get a moment's rest and,' she smiled slightly, 'she's really past retirement age despite what it says in her documents. She's younger than her real age by five years in her documents.'

'How do you know?' Shib couldn't remember what her real age was.

'She told me herself, of course. It was done years ago. I think she's forgotten herself that she's older than she's supposed to be.'

'See if you can persuade her,' he had replied at last.

For he too was fond of Mini; he'd known her when she was a girl in a frock.

Persuading Mini was never easy; it was like a gentle but strenuous tug of war.

'No, Khuku.'

'But I won't hear of anything else.'

For Khuku could be stubborn as well, and Mini discovered she had no answer to that stubbornness.

———

That had been a particularly empty time. For the seven days of the curfew the country had been like a conch whose roar you could hear only if you put your ear to it.

———

'Do you know that Sabita lives here in New Alipore?' said Khuku, after they'd talked about her absent son for about twenty minutes. 'I just spoke to her on the phone the other day. She's put on a lot of weight. Hers is a sad story. Her only son is divorced.'

'Divorced?'

'Yes,' said Khuku, 'his wife left him for his own cousin. Strange things happen these days.'

'What of Anjali?' asked Mini, ruminating.

'I haven't seen her myself. I heard she lives in an ashram in the South. You know she took to wearing saffron and became a sanyasini. Apparently she still remembers me.'

'Of course she would,' said Mini.

In the afternoon, they'd begin discussing their school

again, and their head mistress and deputy head mistress (the one who dressed strangely, because she'd been to England) – 'and the head mistress always loved me,' said Khuku, 'she was always throwing me out of class' – while their conversation meandered and began again. For the twenty-five years in Bombay and Delhi she'd lost touch with most of her school friends. Now, here they were, in Calcutta. And when the conversation went on for too long, and the plot grew too complex, Khuku would fall asleep. Sometimes Mini would doze off first, and Khuku would say, 'You're not listening!' and she would wake up with a start, good-naturedly.

Aᴠᴛᴇʀ Vɪᴅʏᴀsᴀɢᴀʀ Rᴏᴀᴅ had curved right and moved towards the house where *Ganashakti* arrived for distribution, and after the small barricaded grassy triangle there was a by-lane on the left.

In this nameless thoroughfare the boys had begun to set up mikes and wiring, and often at different times of the day stealthy electronic static buzzed and disturbed the lane beneath the other noises. No one knew for certain yet that it was in this by-lane that the performance would take place. But they'd begun to make a stage.

Then a voice said, 'Hello, hello,' and Bhaskar's mother heard it as she was folding a sari. However, she paid it no heed, was not even conscious of it as a separate thing.

This voice continued to say, 'Hello, hello.' The next day it began to say more words, too garbled to be understood from a distance: 'Announce ... country ... a few days from now.'

Two of the men, Jodu and Pyari, had remained silent throughout, notably shy unlike the others; they had been enlisted seemingly at random from the adult literacy class; one was a carpenter and the other worked in a cement factory. They looked quite tired. 'Everyone must take opart,' they were told; for they were all in their way ranged against one nameless enemy. 'What do you think?' they'd been asked; they were approached with a mixture of admonishment and cajoling. 'Dada, will we be able to remember our lines?' said Jodu, the more vocal of the two.

'It's not Tagore you have to memorize,' admonished Bhaskar, and went on to other things.

Gradually they overcame their shyness; convinced themselves they didn't mind at all as long as their wives weren't there to watch them. Jodu was the short one, the one who had more confidence. He took the lead and Pyari followed. It didn't bother them too much that they didn't know what the play was about; these young men came one day, as if in a dream, and told them it was in a good cause, and they believed them. They told them that this letter was pronounced 'kaw', and this one 'khaw', and they repeated the letters after them.

———

Inside a room on the ground floor of a house, Bhaskar and his friends – Sumanta, Nikhilesh, and Mahesh – went over their lines and actions; a few others were drinking tea. Outside, someone kept saying, 'Hello hello check one – two – three—' while inside the flame of Socialism burned and dimmed and burned brightly again; the last of the sunlight fell on the road through a congregation of roofs and solitary antennae; a dog ran swiftly across and crickets began to sing. The proximity of the houses and the little street weighed in on them; this was their poor, true theatre. But, alas, they did not have the ability to concentrate for very long; they drifted out of the play into their own lives. Someone said, 'Bring me some tea,' or 'For God's sake, light a cigarette!'

THEY WOKE, slept, talked. They eked out the days with inconsequential chatter.

Rumours of atrocities in other cities came and went around them. Meanwhile, Nando went out to the market and came back, having pocketed a rupee and fifty paisa for himself.

Until one day Mini persuaded Khuku that she could no longer leave Shantidi by herself, and to reassure her she said, 'As you can see I'm almost a hundred per cent better, Khuku, it's true; I feel stronger than I have in months.' And she gesticulated with an arm, emphatically, to convey what was an essentially incommunicable truth. She gazed at Khuku, to gauge her friend's response from her face.

Earlier that week, she'd been to the nursing home again. By now she had become familiar with the corridor that led to Osteopathy, and the waiting-room in which she and Khuku sat until she was called in. People milled around under the signs saying Osteopathy and Radiology and Cancer Detection for apparently no purpose, coming and going until they sat down down on the chairs: middle-aged women in saris, men in spectacles.

She and Khuku had grown used to its faint electric

lights, its air of being cut off. And the treatment had cost Mini only thirty rupees a visit. Half an hour of the infrared had soothed her arthritis and numbed the leg into the sweetness of acceptance.

E ARLY IN the afternoon on a Tuesday they set out for Madan Chatterjee Lane, where Mini's house was. By half-past three Mini had worn a fresh sari for the journey; folded and put her things into her bag.

Khuku was feeling drowsy because she hadn't taken her nap. 'I'll make up for it in the car,' she said. 'I'll doze off for twenty minutes.' For no reason that could be clearly identified or named, Khuku felt the infinitely reticent and light touch of a sadness, something to do with journeys and roads and people, which she used to experience not infrequently when she was a girl, except that it, and life itself, was much more real then.

No sooner was she in the car than she closed her eyes. She sat in the car, her chin drooping, while the car turned near the corner of a pavement. Fifteen minutes later the noise of the traffic woke her; she said: 'We're still in Beckbagan!'

It took them forty-five minutes to negotiate Lower Circular Road, Chowringhee, the junction before Bentinck Street and finally to pass Mahajati Sadan and to arrive at the small lane on the left. By then, they felt like they'd come to what was probably another city. Just on the right what looked like a deep ditch had been dug in Central Avenue, where actually unfinished work for the underground had been begun and then interrupted. Although the ditch looked almost fearful, there were in fact two children playing and rushing upon it, climbing from one side to the other and disappearing again.

Narrowly the lane opened; only just enough space, like arms reluctantly parted, leaving no room for an embrace to the bosom. Yet the car moved forward into this narrow space, obstructed by handcarts and men, going more and more into the interior, towards the heart, towards a home in the heart.

M UCH WOULD change in the next few months in subtle ways, but much would seem to remain unchanged. And the change was probably only a phase, a development as short-lived as anything else; while what seemed to be in a condition of stasis might actually be shimmering with uncertainty and on the brink of extinction.

And Mini's departure created a gap, a hiatus, that would take time to be replenished again. She had left a vacancy in Khuku's flat, a vague but living memory of her sitting upon a sofa, reading, and it would take time now for Khuku's life to reassert itself. Later, Khuku would hear of Mini's being restricted to her home because of Shantidi's accident, a fall down the stairs and a minor but troublesome fracture. Winter would end, and Mini would be circumscribed by teaching during the day and return-ing home. It was as if life, or history, were a spirit that kept transforming its features, discontented to be one thing at one time.

The change in the weather from late January to early February was small but palpable, a fractional abatement of the dawn's and evening's chill. The winter, crystalline at dawn, smoke-filled in memory, was ending. Then there were the other changes, the larger ones; as the country altered, gradually and almost imperceptibly, from one kind of place to another. Memories died and new ways of life came into being.

Then, in February, Bhaskar's parents began to look for a bride for him in earnest, surreptitiously almost, neither advertising in newspapers nor telling relatives, but sending out signals discreetly.

ALTHOUGH HE knew now that they wouldn't make his plan for Little's work, Shib kept going as if nothing had happened. Once he was in his office, accountants came into his room to ask him to clear up some problem they were having or simply for some advice, and he would help them out – almost minister to them – wondering what his role here was supposed to be. But no real work had been done for days.

His youthfulness (though they knew he was a retired man) had moved the rest of the staff from apathy to something approaching constructiveness. He had come in like a spirit in transit. And he still walked more quickly than most men forty years younger than him.

Again the feeling of peace returned. He could pick up his telephone and ring Khuku if he wanted, but he didn't feel the need to.

He sorted out his files gravely. He was used to being alone, inhabiting his own world: for he was an only child whose mother had died when he was two. Moreover, he had completed a lifetime of looking after others and fending for himself; even Khuku, when he'd first married her, was in many ways helpless; and he had been a sort of shade-giving umbrella to his son, who'd had a happy and extended childhood.

When he'd first come to Calcutta he'd been a young man, twenty years old, and he'd put his name down, Shib Purakayastha, in a register in Calcutta University.

He smiled. Is there an alchemy for making the old new?

'Tea, sir?'

He smiled and shook his head at the man who had asked the question.

The man withdrew.

Two months ago it was that he'd considered with an employee, a marketing manager in this company whose products seldom infiltrated the market, the idea of putting in a fresh advertisement for the company. 'But where?' There was, for instance, a seven-year-old poster with Little's printed upon it in large letters under a railway bridge in the South – day and night the trains rumbled above it and the bridge shuddered – whose paper had peeled off almost entirely, leaving behind, miraculously, only the 'Little's' at the top.

———

Sometimes this man, who had just asked him if he would have tea, brought him lozenges in their new wrappers with Little's printed on both sides. He had ceased to wonder about this company, or what he really did here, or where his salary came from. And Shib had asked to see the lozenges because he was interested in assessing the 'standard' of the product; he'd taken them home to his wife, surprising her by giving her a small full packet. For the story of a working life is also the story of a marriage. She'd put one to the test immediately.

'But it's wonderful!' Khuku had said, absorbed in the

flavour of the lozenge; it reminded her of when she was a child, for the flavour, as it was then, came back to her unchanged; she'd tasted them in Shillong as a girl; and she grew puzzled and anxious trying to understand the reasons for Little's decline.

Each time a state- or government-supported company closed down, it was like a death-knell that no one heard. And Shib heard it these days.

It was only after months that people realized that a company was gone. A product disappeared from the market, or it might be bought over by a Marwari businessman and sold as if nothing had happened. And as if removed from all this, in a constricted space, the office window looked out onto the stunted outgrowth of Dum Dum.

But in his spare time, Khuku's husband had decided to put aside some money in shares; he had a premonition that there was a change at hand. All his life, he had worked in a company, and had had no taste for business or speculation; he had been a cautious and qualified professional. But now, four years after retirement, some demon seemed to have seized him; when he was not watching television, he wore small, focused reading glasses that sat low on the bridge of his nose, and fussed over papers and forms. Now, with economic deregulation and a freedom that, in theory, had never existed before, there was the prospect of a rainbow-deluge of collaborations and all kind of opportunities coming to the surface. And Little's would then be a thing of yesterday.

Cautiously he decided to invest some money in the Mutual Fund and uncharacteristically to buy a few shares in a company that made biscuits, and in another one that made shoes. Now, in the last quarter of his life, a business acumen and speculative curiosity, long suppressed in the interests of his managerial skills, began to come into play, and also a silent, watchful interest in political issues, and he began to peruse the papers with more than usual thoroughness. His gaze and concentration as he absorbed the curve and emerging shape of the time were intent.

All was silence around him. At odd moments lost in thoughts on these matters he could be found humming to himself. No one but Khuku, and Bablu, who was not here, knew that he sang. From what little could be heard of that singing voice it would seem that it was a small, high-pitched one, at variance with the quiet dignity of his persona, not very sure of itself. It skirted around the difficult portions and paraphrased the tune rather than sang it; but it was a strange, lonely rehearsal to itself (often in response to a song that Khuku had just sung) rather than meant for others to hear. When Khuku overheard him, she would say to her husband – 'What? what? are you singing? I see you're not lacking in courage!' – and discouraged, he would stop.

WOMEN'S MEMORIES of their husbands' working life are radically but subtly different from their husbands' own, and the same must be true of their retirement. It's like seeing something from the other side. Of course, Khuku felt lonely when Shib was in his office; and always had done. But, then, during the curfew, when shops and offices and everything else had been closed – ten days of nothing happening – she'd had her wish come true, and Shib at home with her for twenty-four hours of the day.

It had been a mixed blessing, this enforced, artificial reunion. It was as if a train they'd been on had halted somewhere unexpectedly and they'd been forced to take a holiday. She'd found that he wasn't interested in discussing what was happening at all – the riots, the anger; more interested in re-reading old copies of the *Statesman* which he'd accumulated during the last week in a drawer. How little concerned he was about the silence outside, in which the sound of a single car horn became disconcerting, as he sat all morning reading! Neglecting to shave, even; a grey stubble appearing on his cheeks.

The truth is, he was not used to being at home. And with Bablu away they were less like a couple than a pair of lodgers.

Then, gradually, the heap of newspapers by his side of

the bed had grown, the small alley by the bed littered with papers, as if he were undertaking some sort of research. And his going to the toilet three times in the silence of the night, the sound of the flush nudging her deep in her sleep; she'd begun to worry whether there was anything wrong with his prostate. Any sign of abnormality made her worry and wonder, and this new silence outside and proximity within brought to her awareness what she probably hadn't noticed before. She listened to him breathe at night. Many nights she spent not sleeping, but thinking and awake.

Once the curfew had ended he'd gone out into the world and bought oranges. But it had been a great blunder. On returning home, Khuku pointed out that they were, from the way they peeled and tasted, those terrible sour mutations that resembled oranges, kinoos. She derided him for his lack of discrimination. 'What!' Shib said. 'But I *told* him I want oranges!' Indignation, however, could not change the kinoos into oranges. Life had begun again.

And then there were only two days left for that performance.

'No, it's not a *famous* group; I've never heard of them before. But it's a nice name. You feel you *must* have heard of them.'

'That's right.'

The two, aunt and niece, were desultorily discussing that frayed but bright entity, Bhaskar's theatre troupe; for this late manifestation of the artistic bent was worth commenting on. Yet one of Khuku's elder brothers, now dead, had written poetry, in rhyme and in blank verse, in twelve-line sonnets, in a marvellous phase between the age of eighteen and twenty, and had even had one poem published in *Desh*, and that copy had been circulated in at least five houses.

Another brother, Pulu, had done a stage adaptation of an unadaptable Sukumar Ray poem when he was a young man in Shillong, using all his four- and five-year-old nieces and nephews and his sisters-in-law in the cast (that was when Khuku was in London, rainswept and with six hours of sunlight, with Shib, who was still a student, and it had been described to her in a letter; and she'd known the strangeness of being in another country that she could not recognize if she looked out of the window and have the sense of her own country return to her from a description).

And it was now, a few days before this street-play, that it occurred to Khuku that her family had always been full of ne'er-do-wells, each one doing exactly what he pleased, and if Pulu hadn't been brought to England in 1959 with Shib's help he'd still be wheeling and dealing in second-hand cars in Shillong (which is what he'd been doing when he'd had that play enacted – a major success – when her nephew and niece Moni and Beena – Borda's children – and India itself had been ridiculously, helplessly young). These ne'er-do-wells were somehow provided for by Providence. And she thought of that family and realized that the bonds of relations surrounding it, radiating across and scattered through this city and elsewhere, was finally coming to an end, and she unexpectedly grew absorbed in its memories.

'And they're just a handful of boys,' said Puti. 'I wonder how Bhola mama copes with them.'

'He's indulgent – towards all his children, I'd say.'

'But too much indulgence isn't good, is it?' said Puti, mother of a son, Mohit, who was so responsible at fourteen that he sometimes even gave advice to his parents.

At this moment, Bhaskar was witnessing the construction of a stage in a by-lane off Vidyasagar Road.

They'd arranged about seventy-five chairs, in rows.

———

Borda's elder daughter in Golf Green was among those that had heard of the performance. She, Beena, lived with her parents, and went to work each morning with the air of one about to perform, once again, an indispensable task. The rest of the family almost forgot about her at times, as they forgot those with less than ordinary fortunes; until they thought about her again in a wave of passing sympathy. She was planning to go – 'Dear Bhaskar's play': she could not miss it.

For she was something of an enthusiast of the arts herself, taught Tagore songs rather tunelessly but insistently to small children who lived in her block. The children, whom she gave lessons at no fixed time of the day, quite adored her singing. Her surname was Mitra, a word that had come to have sad, paradoxical music to it (she had decided not to change her husband's name, from whom she had separated eleven years ago). Fortunately she earned a small salary teaching at the primary level at an orphanage in which she taught English to thirty destitute children in a class. In her more lonely and sentimental moments she often felt that these children were like the children she didn't have; but who, having seen her as a young woman of twenty would have suspected that her life would take this particular shape when she was forty-five? Bhaskar's own cousin, Khuku's and Bhola's niece, she was no longer noticed, a shadow, like other shadows, enfolded within this city.

THE SOUND of the radio came from outside; and from a side-table Mini picked up her spectacles; it was morning and the moment of waking; the consciousness which meant a return to these sounds of the building and further away the noises of Chitpur Road.

Splashes of water fell upon the hard floor; Shantidi was in the bath; they fell, again, and again. And here was the day's paper, lying on the floor, by the door. And in the cupboard next to the door was a small container with plastic boards with dates upon them which had to be reshuffled every day; Mini would pause and change the date by hand as if not entirely convinced that it was another day until she had done so; then she would bend to pick the paper up.

———

Five sisters and brothers in that family: Mini and Shantidi, and the three brothers, Shyamal, Chanchal, and the eldest, whom they used to call Dadamoni. They had grown up in a place called Puran Lane in Sylhet, a flat area with a longish lane of houses, not a great distance from a market, and which must have been in the East of the town since the sun seemed to rise on that side.

Their father had been a soft-spoken nondescript man; where he came from was no more clear; the circumstances of his marriage to Mini's mother too were now forgotten. What was remembered was his conversation and his uprightness, and the walks he used to take to Khuku's mother's house from time to time, and how she, widowed, would turn to this gentle man for advice. He – there were thousands like him – had died at the age of fifty-eight, which at that time was considered an acceptable age for death; Mini was sixteen years old. Their mother had gone back to the village a few years later and died there. Their lives existed only in their surviving children's memories and sometimes not even there; it was as if they had been banished into some darker place or retreated there of their own will; and their presence had been so subtle in life, so unremarkable, that words could no longer translate them into existence. They were gone, but would return, without questions, to their children's minds repeatedly. Then, after the mother's death, Mini's elder brother had taken on the responsibilities of the family in an ordinary but godlike way. He, 'Dadamoni', had looked after them as if they were his children; like Shyamal and Mini, he wore spectacles, and like them he had a hoarse voice.

Then the upheaval came, and friends, brothers, teachers, magistrates, servants, shopkeepers were all uprooted, as if released slowly, sadly, by the gravity that had tied them to the places they had known all their life, released from an old orbit. They had awaited it with more than apprehension; but when it came they hardly noticed it. The votes were counted after the referendum; their country was gone; first they went back to the village where their mother had died. After two months they packed their things and took a train to Guwahati and then a bus to Shillong, the landscape, over six hours, changing slowly from plains to hills.

Later, Dadamoni came to Calcutta with his brothers and sisters and rented a flat not far from where they were now; and took a job as a sales representative in a chemicals company. They'd lost their home; but there was the silent, incommunicable excitement of beginning anew in what was now their own country. When they walked down the road and saw a large hoarding advertising Dutta Chemicals, they felt proud as if at a secret knowledge. (They hardly remarked later on the demise of Dutta Chemicals; it had gone out of business in the Seventies, but their lives were so different by then they had hardly noticed it.)

When Khuku spent three days in Calcutta on her way to England in 1955, to marry Shib, Mini'd been living in a lane with Dadamoni, Shantidi, Chanchal, and Shyamal in the rented flat. Khuku then told Mini how beautiful the city seemed to her, for this was her first visit here; and urged Mini to marry. She had someone in mind, she said, a young man called Kalidas Sengupta who worked in an advertising firm. For those three days she pursued the subject of Mini's marriage, to Mini's slight embarrassment. Then she was gone for six years.

Shantidi came out now, half-blind with the bath. She was cold.

When he was only forty-two years old, Dadamoni died. The day before he died of a heart attack, he'd had a meal of ilish fish, a noble specimen caught from the Ganga whose virtues he commended as he slowly sorted the bones in his mouth. Later, when the pains had started, he'd thought, at first, that it was indigestion. And in less than two years, Chanchal, who was running a catering business, contracted tuberculosis; and tuberculosis was still incurable in those days. With Dadamoni's death (his photograph hung on the wall in the smaller room) everything changed with a slow momentum that they did not fully grasp; and their destinies turned out to be different from what even a year ago they believed they might have been. The possibility of Shantidi's and Mini's marriage became more remote; and then, they did not know exactly when, it no longer remained a possibility. In a way they were left innocent, like children, never to know what one part of life was, not particularly worried by their ignorance, with an inexhaustible core of freshness and even romance, touched and changed only by time's attrition and the uncontainability of their own affections. They gradually stopped thinking and talking about it as one stops thinking about things whose meaning one outgrows or transcends. Meanwhile, Khuku and Shib returned to Calcutta from England as, strangely, touchingly, husband and wife, Shib armed with rare and desirable qualifications of which Khuku was proud as if she had taken the exams; and their first and only child was born in a nursing home in South Calcutta. Everything had happened in Khuku's life at an abnormally slow pace: married at the age of thirty, she was giving birth to this son after years of trying. Khuku was thirty-seven years old, and Shib forty, his hair already half grey, but his face strikingly young.

A sound from outside, like something beating against metal. There it was, again and again.

Mini would sometimes remember the two years they'd spent in Calcutta after returning from England. Bablu learning to walk, taking his first steps in the courtyard of their house in New Alipore; Khuku become plump and motherly compared to the thin woman she'd been before leaving for England, her hair dark and thick, fanning out behind her unmanageably; proud of her husband's new job in a company that made bread. She was still singing of course; she was looking for a music teacher to teach her new songs not in her repertoire. And Mini was working in the school. She still wore almost the same kind of saris as she did now, pale, with a thin coloured border, and tied her hair in a bun.

Other noises flowed in, between the metal being beaten, as if all material things in the neighbourhood were gradually being transformed into sound.

Then Khuku and Shib had moved to Delhi, and, for twenty-five years, Mini would see Khuku only when she visited Calcutta once a year, usually in the summer.

Not long after Dadamoni's death, they'd been allocated this flat in the New Municipal Corporation Building.

Mini walked towards the table in front of the fridge and poured herself a glass of water.

At one end was the small kitchen. In the centre was a space where the table was kept, and a clothes-line hung from one end to another; and to the left was a window covered by a wire gauze. The walls enclosed a medium-sized space that was partially filled with light.

The obscure lines of the gauze had become dark and sometimes a feather which had been stuck there might remain there until it had been worn away. That window opened onto the intricate jumble of lanes and terraces of North Calcutta, receding and approaching, mirroring and leading towards each other, and towards Girish Park and Vivekananda Road.

Although Mini's age was reduced by five years in her documents she was due to retire in about two years.

The two sisters were tenants here, although there had been talk for some time (always listened to with interest, always exciting a small ripple of speculation) that people who had lived in their flats for more than fifteen years would be given ownership. Among the tenants themselves there had been a tentative self-appraisal: 'Yes, I've been here for seventeen years'; or 'It's nineteen years this year.' The numbers were like a revelation. Time suddenly seemed to have passed quickly, even forgivingly. Each year for the last five years an official said: 'It'll be this year.'

Until nine years ago Mini and Shantidi used to lived in this flat with their younger brother Shyamal and his family. He used to work as a junior manager in a small company; all three of them going out each day to work; reuniting at tea-time in the afternoon; Shantidi and Mini beginning to cook a meal in the kitchen at seven o'clock. That was their life after Dadamoni's and Chanchal's death. Then his sisters began looking for someone for him to marry; they discovered Lalita, younger daughter of a Professor Hiren Shome of Sylhet, who was beginning life as a schoolteacher herself. Shyamal and Lalita were married, and she moved into the tiny flat, and the second room on the right, near the kitchen, became their bedroom. A few months later, a trivial incident caused a misunderstanding between her and Mini and Shantidi. There was nothing unnatural about that: for they had to live, eat, cook, and breathe and the newly-weds lead their married life in the same small space. Yet that was Calcutta then, and everything was possible and probable in their lives; and they were grateful for the flat. While Mini went out to work, Shantidi made sweets, boiling and condensing milk, frying things. Then Lalita had two children, both boys; but the quarrels between their mother and their aunts continued. The quarrels did not affect the boys' relations with Mini and Shantidi; they loved and harassed and disconcerted the two women who were gradually ageing. And it was lovely to have children growing up in the flat, with tricycles and Ludo boards coming in the way, and rubber balls bouncing off beneath the bed.

Nevertheless things seemed to go on indefinitely with their portion of affection and unpleasantness and joy.

But what was begun in a certain way never arrived at its expected conclusion. So there was almost no surprise when nine years ago Shyamal and his family moved to a house in a different part of the city. And the two sisters were left to lead their lives in this building.

———

'Didi, I'm off,' said Mini, before setting out for the school – matter-of-factly, as if she was off to attend a political rally.

She was wearing a fresh sari; her small handbag and a cloth bag hung from her shoulder.

'I might go out myself,' called Shantidi. 'I'm waiting for that girl.' A part-time maidservant came every day at about eleven o'clock to cook meals.

Mini went down the badly lit stairs and emerged then into the bright compound and faced the old building opposite hers, such a faithful mirror-image of her own and yet strangely different; the small first-floor flats with clothes-lines by their windows, the windows covered with a wire gauze, the pipe running down one corner of the wall. It took her about two minutes to get to the main gates and leave the buildings behind her.

As she approached the gates she was greeted from behind a gauze net by a woman with a child in her arms on a ground-floor veranda.

'Minidi, when did you come back?' Her smile was partly obscured by the gauze, and then she emerged into the open part of the veranda, almost becoming another person, the baby unconcerned in her arms, staring tranquilly at the sky between the tops of the buildings.

'How is little Bijon?' asked Mini, her slight smile echoing the woman's.

She had held so many children in her arms, here, in these buildings, and they had gone. This, these buildings, was home and not home; the country she'd left behind in her youth was home and not home; where you went later was not home either; the baby, though it did not know it, must end up making a journey, must end up somewhere else. Her feelings about home must remain painful and blurred to the end of her life. She took the child in her arms, unprotesting, then gave it back. 'It seems longer than it has been really. But,' her voice half-concealed by sounds around her, as if all you could do was become a voice among other voices, 'I had a rest and lost track of time.'

'We were wondering,' said the woman, 'but I can now see it's done you good. There's a shine on your face; I know.'

Pigeons rose suddenly into the sky between the buildings; their conversation evaporated rather than ended; the child began to make sounds as if it had had enough.

And now, with enough time still on her hands, she stepped into the lane.

Hindustani and Bihari tradesmen lived here, on the left of the gates. They did not notice Mini as she walked past. They were like a tribe that clung to its own impenetrable rituals, curiously unconcerned by the public gaze; their forefathers must have moved here a hundred years ago; it seemed they hardly slept; late into the night, sometimes, one could hear the men singing devotionals, and they must be the first humans to be woken by the sunlight at dawn. The lane moved on to the right of the gates of the New Municipal Corporation Buildings and after dissecting, at right angles, the narrow lane that led out to Central Avenue, proceeded towards an old 'palace'. Between shops there were landlords' houses, ornate husks, in which no one lived. But no, someone *did* live in there, for there, across the enclosure of the courtyard, surrounded by the theatre of balconies, doors, and rather beautiful, shadowy stairwells, was the mundane parabola of a clothesline with washing left out to dry. There were little goats in the lane, and, by the side of families, children who were older than babies but not quite teenagers sometimes turned erratic cartwheels, as if they were celebrating something.

As she approached the corner of the small lane, she passed the sweet shop in which business would swell noticeably in the afternoon, before four o'clock, before tea-time, when the daily cargo of sweets and savouries came in. And then their vivid smell would overwhelm the other smells in the immediate proximity of the shop.

BEENA HAD gone to see the play being enacted; Khuku couldn't go. That evening, it was suddenly done. With the performance of the street-play over, however it might have been tangential or in the background, and the set dismantled, the larger family shattered and became, temporarily, little islands, each with its own memories and pastimes. All that joined them tenuously in their different places were the rumours of something like war. They read the headlines each day, in newspapers that were already old when they'd finished reading them, of a country that had turned upon itself, without really being able to take them in: 'Where hate comes in a communal garb'; then the smaller headings: 'Seven killed in violence'; or the same sentence, with eight substituting for seven. Was it really as bad as that? There were these small eruptions and they would hear of them and feel an almost unseemly thrill. There would be a photograph sometimes, of people sitting in a railway station, under a roof like an immense tent with their children and possessions, a child half asleep, looking like the nomads of old, suddenly uprooted, without an address, waiting to depart from the city.

Sleepy-eyed sometimes, sometimes wide awake, they, especially Khuku, would spend the morning reading.

They did not know what the appropriate reaction should be: shock; a certain sense of being vindicated; or a lingering sense of unpleasantness. At times Khuku would surprise herself by thinking of Mini and wonder how she was.

Here, a Muslim butcher had been found near the bypass with his skull shattered, blood on his forehead and face. No one knew why he had been killed; there had been a quarrel, a group of people. There was silence while the police looked into it. The man's face appeared in a photograph, dead, his eyes closed and lips parted, part of his eye and cheekbone obscured by blood.

He seemed to sleep uncomfortably, his lips parted and eyes closed.

But there were always minor surprises. In the personal column, under Death, next to Choudhuri, Mrinalini, was: Passed away peacefully on 19th January, at the age of 77, mourned by two daughters, Priya and Tuktuk, son, Bimal, and daughter-in-law, Soumya, as well as grandchildren Joy and Sharmistha. Ceremony on Tuesday 22nd. All welcome.

Khuku hadn't noticed this; but Shib saw it. The little obituary, meaningless to almost everyone, a coded message to the few it would nudge towards recognition, signified a pause before the year set off confusedly again in a predetermined direction.

'Mrinalini Choudhuri – that name sounds familiar,' said Shib, ordinarily so bad with names.

'Obviously it's familiar,' said Khuku, preoccupied but peremptory. 'It's Banidi, that's who it is, Didi's friend in college; oh, Banidi, don't you remember!' becoming impatient.

Names; one name suggesting another. As the mist

began to clear the shock sank in. Mrinalini Choudhuri was Banidi; she had come to their house last year with her younger daughter who was in her forties, saying to Khuku, as if it were a great joke, 'Khuku! I haven't seen you in *years*!' No doubt a little pleased that she'd outlived her friend, she still lovely like a long-living creeper that had coiled itself around the earthly and thrown up in the evening a new blossom. And she spoke to Khuku, her friend's younger sister, about ten years younger than her, as if she was a girl: 'No, no, I won't hear of it, let's hear that song, Khuku.' Inexplicably they'd lost touch for twenty years and thus there was that breathlessness on seeing each other again.

'It must be Banidi; who else would it be? We used to think she was quite pretty when she was young, you know; dark, but pretty. Why do you ask?'

'WHAT WILL it be today, Didi?' Suleiman asked, as he sat down to tune the tabla. Yet something about his manner always made her impatient.

She decided to sing a love-song she had learnt as a child.

> *The moon smiles without a hindrance,*
> *Light overflows.*
> *O flower, O tuberose,*
> *Pour forth the nectar of your fragrance.*

The nectar of your fragrance – the swooning perfume of an imaginary tuberose! But the song and its words had the innocence of an alphabet, learnt when only sound, and before meaning, had entered the consciousness. She no longer remembered who had taught her this song (the tabla rang, bell-like, as Suleiman struck it with his finger-tips); it might have been one of her elder brothers, or a relative, or she might have picked it up from a record. Songs were common currency in the small towns, and in Sylhet they travelled from radios into the interiors of houses and they used to learn them by whatever means possible. Sometimes they would hear a visiting relative singing them in the bath and they had the gift, almost a desperate one, of remembering a tune from these audible snatches. Songs were meant to be stored and collected; people had a large or small 'stock' of songs.

> *The blue sky's forehead*
> *Is smeared with sandal,*
> *And the pair of swans that belong to the forest*
> *Of words have spread their wings.*

She sang these lines again, for she hadn't got them quite right the first time. After their father's death, their mother had sold the gramophone while she was selling other things that belonged to them. Later, whenever they wanted to listen to the gramophone, they would borrow it from Shib's family, who were rich landowners who did not keep too close a track on their belongings, and they would keep it and a stack of records with them for days.

It had been a strange, an impossible childhood. Their father dead, their mother trying to look after them all, and they – the three youngest ones, Pulu, Bhola, and Khuku – brought up, in effect, by the older sister, who had died last year, an older brother, who had died in Shillong two years ago, another older brother, who had died more than sixty years ago, when he was only thirty years old, of an incurable heart disease – three tyrants – and Borda.

Khuku had longed to sing as a child; but it was Bhola who was always singing when they were children. So Khuku waited shyly in the background as a girl should. Their elder sister bought Bhola a harmonium, but Bhola was too impatient to sit and play it; and it was Khuku, not Bhola, who learnt how to play.

It was an L-shaped house, whose inner and outer dark declivities were indelibly etched within her, to which they'd moved a year after their father had died, their mother taking charge of everything, and there she would often practise on the veranda. But she began practising seriously only when she was in Shillong, sometimes early in the morning, going into another room so as not to wake the others, and her brothers would tease her and call her 'Bijonbala Ghosh Dastidar!' after the famous classical singer. Yet she had an intent and determination that seemed to see far into the future.

Almost no one had the privilege of listening to her these days except her husband and Suleiman or those who happened to be near, including Jochna and Nando. Not infrequently her old records were played on the radio, and that voice ringing as it used to be would fill the air.

WHEN SHE finished the song, she began another one immediately, almost impatiently. And all at once she noticed Suleiman before her.

All of last month had been an embarrassment to him; as if he'd been transformed into a creature of peculiar and noticeable appearance. And it was as if he was surprised that he was still here, leading the same life he'd led before in Park Circus two months ago.

As for Khuku, she was often in a state of irritation. Only recently she'd been woken up again by the azaan, and at first she had thought it was a mosquito humming near her ear. It grew louder, and then faded, and then grew louder again; its note swelled faintly and then diminished, just as when a mosquito hovers above one in indecision. Then she realized what it was. Where is it coming from? she wondered. It must be Park Circus, from one of those lanes above which the minarets rose. It reminded her that there were altogether too many Muslims around her. Sometimes, in the afternoon, the sound hovered in the middle air, and, if she were passing by in the car, she could sometimes hear two different voices at different pitches; as one came closer, they filled the air.

'Is it necessary for all the world to hear it?' she had asked later.

Suleiman had explained himself and his faith apologetically, the tablas balefully silent before him. 'It is the word of God,' he said, shamefaced and tender about this perpetual nuisance.

See how stubborn they are, she thought; and just the other day they were quaking with fear.

It was more than three weeks since that conversation had taken place.

'Which song, Didi?' he asked.

She did not answer; not because she did not mean to, but because she was asking precisely the same question of herself, and thus had not heard him. She began a familiar song:

> *Lost heart*
> *On a verdant road*
> *I gather strewn flowers*
> *By myself*

Park Circus; Shamsul Huda Haq Road. A pharmacy and a sweet shop at its entrance. Only a twenty minutes' walk from Khuku's house.

During their festivals, sweets made of semolina were left in platters and distributed; they prayed here; marriages were made; they had their own butchers' and tailors' shops. They had their own school for the blind and their madrassas. Children and women in saris and in burkhas, maulvis and music teachers and private tutors and businessmen all mingling under storeys that were heaped one on top of the other.

I T WAS not many days after the performance and already a meeting was arranged between Bhola's family and the Duttas. 'The Duttas are a good family,' said Bhaskar's mother, though she did not know the Duttas. The Duttas had a daughter. When, at the end of the month, the meeting with the 'girl' and her parents was set to take place at an open-air café near Salt Lake, Bhaskar, oddly, seemed both indifferent and co-operative and full of nimble self-assurance.

That very day, however, he'd said he'd have to go to a meeting. Bhaskar's mother had met this observation with coolness. 'Go, then. We'll be able to make another arrangement.' The café was new and appeared largely unfrequented and lit by large lanterns and set against a lake. Had it been designed in its flickering anonymity specifically with meetings such as this one in mind? Bhaskar wondered. The bypass leading to the airport ran next to it; and at this time the bypass was illuminated principally by headlights. Bhaskar's mother, her sari drawn around her to protect herself from the breeze that blew towards them from the dark, asked for Gold Spot (because it was a fairly long time since she'd had a soft drink); so did Piyu; but Bhola and the girl's parents said 'Thums Up' to the waiter. The darkness that surrounded them had in the morning been water and land and a fragment of sky. The drinks eventually came towards them on a tray and gravitated above the table. There were no other customers except a couple in the distance, who had no doubt come here for their own reasons, looked recently married, and kept glancing, whether with curiosity or displeasure it was difficult to tell, at the two families. Suddenly, taking Bhaskar aback, Bhola offered that Bhaskar and Anusuya, for whose sake this rendezvous had been arranged, sit at another table so that they could 'talk amongst themselves'. Heavily Bhaskar got up; lightly Anusuya, though she was overweight, got up; and made for the neighbouring table, as if they would become invisible to the others once they sat there. Bhaskar had decided that he would not, could not marry this girl. She reminded him of a schoolfriend he used to have, a boy called Anilesh. But he was determined to be polite, as polite as he ever was; and he almost felt a surge of affection for her when she asked the waiter for ice-cream. Bhaskar sipped Thums Up non-committally from a straw. They must have grown up simultaneously, in schools not far from each other; and now they were both in the twilight world of being unmarried. They seemed resigned and happy to be enjoying their orders.

'What do you think?' asked Bhola on the way back.

'What should I think?' said Bhaskar. 'We didn't speak. She was busy eating ice-cream.'

A ND BHASKAR, after a gap of five days, resumed going to the factory. He left agitated and late in the morning after a meal of fish and rice.

The factory – time had not dulled the route to it nor made it easier – took an hour and a half to get to by car; it meant crossing the Howrah Bridge; then passing through places that were neither towns nor outposts, but that had names; and negotiating a bad road. Neither tree nor bird in sight, nothing but the little stalls one left behind with pictures of Krishna in them; this was the road to Howrah. By train, it took a little less time.

This was the journey his father had made for the last twenty-five years, the journey he'd made when Bhaskar and Manik and Piyu were at school, their heads bent separately over books, and their mother at home. Its frequency and purpose had, by now, after all these years, diminished, the trip almost become ordinary, a repeated ritual rather than an ambition. And Bhaskar too had now embarked upon this sketchy but indelible route.

Part of the reason for the aggravation of Bhaskar's backache, it had to be admitted, was the jolts and bumps of the drive. The Municipal Corporation, it seemed, had no money to repair these roads and would have none in the near future. The interconnected, anonymous roads, adorned at intervals by small tea-shops, one half-defined vista giving way to another, shrank at last and resolved itself into something concrete and real and small, into this factory that had always been there. Its gates presented itself along a lane only wide enough to accommodate one car at a time.

The larger companies around it had left, but it and others like it had remained and made of this place their special habitat. It was Lord Vishwakarma who looked after this company and the cranes that it made and who looked after its neighbours and their small range of products.

And yet of late Bhola and Bhaskar had been discussing in a slightly emotional way the effect liberalization would have on their company. For new times bring new and unforeseen exigencies. 'It'll be difficult for us to survive,' said Bhola with satisfaction. 'The big ones will go in for collaborations and mergers. And the small ones will be pushed out by multinationals.' They made gloomy and extreme predictions.

———

Here South Calcutta receded; homes, children, mothers, servants were replaced by men in dirty overalls wandering about in the workshed. Without explanation, the machines hummed and rattled. In other factories nearby, machines hummed and rattled as well for the purposes of a tiny but persistent line of production.

There was a calendar on the wall of the 'office'; an old map; near the workshop, a small shrine.

Bhaskar oversaw what everyone else was doing;

checked if any fresh orders had come through; dialled several phone numbers for fresh orders.

'The whole world's in a recession,' he said. And indeed it was.

Then he made a few more phone calls.

———

This company had been founded by a group of friends, some of whom, like Bhola, had given up jobs to pool their resources into the business, others who had been waiting to make a beginning in some sort of enterprise. That was a time when many middle-class people decided to start small businesses. All of Bhola's partners lived, as it happened, in South Calcutta, not far from each other.

Then the daily journeys began, exultant at first, routine later.

As a business grows or fails, the families of its employees and owners live out their separate destinies. Children grow up over a time that seems longer than it will in retrospect; wives age subtly; they seem young and unchanged for a considerable period of time; men visit the factory and the business enters the bloodstream.

———

Two years after his marriage, Bhola had decided to leave his job and put the money he had received as a gift from his father-in-law into starting this business. His father-in-law himself was an inspiration; a stern man who, through acumen rather than sophistication, had made his enterprise a success; and there was no reason why Bhola and his partners couldn't do what his father-in-law had done.

The father-in-law (dead for thirteen years), whose name had been Radhanath Das – all his products bore the legend 'Das' – had personally been aghast at Bhola's decision.

The partners had intended to contribute something to the country: cranes, and other nuts and bolts of the manufacturing industry. For they were civil engineers, not Marwaris and traders; the country needed them; and there would be big money in it and great demand for it; the country needed dams, bridges, roads and pylons as it grew...

The name they came up with for the factory, Goodforce Literod, was a judicious composite of English words; and Literod became the brand name of a pulley they manufactured.

They produced calendars every year, simple dignified squares with a sheaf of dates attached, and the name Goodforce Literod imprinted upon them, the calendars as much announcing this name as the year they were produced in. Each year, the calendars and that name had their rebirth. It was as if the calendars, whose pages so quickly became ragged, gave the company a legitimacy.

It was during the years of the Naxals that the company went bankrupt. A protracted abeyance began, in which the business brought in nothing, no income, and when it became a symbol of some specific but not easily grasped meaning; it was at this point that the business finally became more than a business, and became a way of life, a definition of the existence of the families that had invested their lives in it. Each morning Bhola's children saw their father going to work, wearing a shirt, trousers, and shoes, although something in them knew he was not going to work.

Yet the name – Goodforce Literod Ltd. – still possessed its music for the children.

Most of the partners had died over the last fifteen years. The factory remained a husk of its first intentions.

Naturally it did not seem that Manik, Bhola's younger son, would ever return to Calcutta and have anything to do with the company. Recently he'd written from Germany that he wanted to study management in America once he'd graduated, which was a very wise thing to do.

Yet – unexpectedly – the company had been functioning for the last two years with a tepid body-warmth, something approaching a normal temperature: and no one knew or could explain why. It was as if the dead partners had, from another world, bestowed their hopes and benedictions upon it.

And each year there was the Vishwakarma Puja. And all members and friends of the family who'd been invited would set out in their cars after filling the tanks with forty litres of petrol, towards Howrah. Though the last cook, whose fragrant preparations of goat's meat and fish-head dal were well known, had died two years ago of cholera, the present cook too had a reputation. For an hour and a half they would travel, to go to the factory in Howrah and eat at the Vishwakarma feast.

But Bhaskar's joining the factory had been seen by others with bemusement and surprise; for it was not as much an entry into the world of business as an escape from it. Why should a young man, unless he had no serious ambition in life, or no choice, want to join a company that was already a ghost of itself? His parents tried not to have to think about the answer to this question. But for Bhaskar, who, after graduating with a second-class commerce degree, and rather desultorily, for a period, studying Cost Accountancy – for Bhaskar, who, afterwards, had moved restlessly from job to temporary job, it had meant a familiar place to go to; it meant not being swallowed up in the orbit of temporary sales work for large companies; and, most importantly, his pride would not be challenged, for he would not work under anyone except his father and with his father's old friends. He gave himself, thus, whole-heartedly to securing fresh orders. He went off to meet Marwari traders; he went to Ranchi to confer with representatives of small companies. He tasted the food in various small towns.

W HEN BHOLA came back to India from Germany he
was only twenty-eight years old; he had no idea
then he'd go into business. He had gone on a course of
technical training; and he was married within a year of
his return, when he was twenty-nine. Bhaskar's mother
was nineteen years old then, barely a woman, and she was
still – it was heard – studying for her BA. But her student
life ended next year, the first year of her marriage, when
she found she had failed her BA because she hadn't
worked hard enough for her English exam; tears flowed
down her cheeks. And Bhola patted her lovingly on the
back. The English language ever eluded her and then,
graciously, came to bother her not at all.

Thereafter, on failing her BA, she, who had little
interest in books, would devote her sporadic but avid
reading habits to women's magazines, and, as she grew
older, to Ramakrishna's *Kathamrita* (which her mother
used to once read) for its queer parables and homilies; for
she often found her mind turning to things that were
holy. She had married Bhola solely because her father
had decided it should be so; a German-trained engineer
counted for a great deal in those days. Bhola's family were
secretly disappointed, although Bhola's wife came, as it

turned out, from a rich business family; but they would have preferred a background with more pedigree, and perhaps a fairer bride. From Assam, Bhola's elder sister, the one they called Didi, came in a train for the wedding; Khuku came in a plane from Delhi.

DURING THE first two years of his married life, he and his wife quarrelled frequently because they often misunderstood each other. But he had a job that was secure, a furnished flat; he had a good beginning in Calcutta.

It is useless to speculate what his life and the lives of his wife and his children might have been like had he kept his job. But he had left it one day on an impulse, ready to listen to no one else, and they vacated the apartment, and moved to a small flat on Swinhoe Street. From there, later, they went to Fern Road, where, probably, Bhaskar was conceived. Below their flat, two doors away, there was a jeweller's, with a collapsible gate and a fat man in a dhuti and cap leaning behind a counter. Finally, they came to Vidyasagar Road.

After Bhaskar's birth (his eyes were so large and dark that they seemed to be outlined with kohl), his mother suffered from a brief but acute spell of depression, such as is common to women after the experience of childbirth. She even wanted to go home; it seemed, strangely, that she could take no more of the marriage. A few days later the depression disappeared and she never spoke of it again.

Such were their lives' inconsequential beginnings.

AND THEY had social obligations that kept them all
occupied early that February. It was a dance with
complex steps; they went to a wedding; they had to go to
Banidi's funeral, she who had died unexpectedly; they
visited one of Bhola's friends, whom he'd almost lost touch
with; a meeting was arranged with a family in a little flat
off Lansdowne Road, to see another 'girl' for Bhaskar. Her
father was a widower: her mother had died of cancer.

Bhola had decided secretly that he must not dwell on
Bhaskar's politics or even politics at all (a difficult renun-
ciation) during the meeting for the sake of a smooth
passage to marriage. Possibly he was going to be a little
disingenuous, but a little disingenuousness didn't count.

Bhaskar would put on some weight after these visits;
for he ate whatever was offered to him. It didn't matter
whether he was hungry or not; he believed he should
profit in some way from these occasions; it was a habit
he'd had since he was a child.

For many days now, Bhola had been trying to arrange
another meeting with a 'party', but Bhaskar had lapsed
easily again into a state of indifference. They showed him

photographs; but he was never at home! When they put their questions to him directly he mumbled his replies. It was not that he didn't care; he was twenty-eight years old; and he experienced an acute absence at times by his side. But it was as if his recent eloquence on politics had left him inarticulate about personal matters; and he had a profound fear that he would not find a bride to his liking. Which girl would marry someone who did not have a well-settled job with chances of promotion in an established company – at the very least? It was to conceal these fundamental and unspoken doubts that he commanded his parents, 'Do what you want, then. And don't wait for my permission. Frankly I have nothing to say on the matter; and when have you listened to me, anyway.'

———

They had gone to the house in the lane off Lansdowne Road early that month. They consulted a shabby calendar, saw that the date had arrived. Bhaskar hadn't returned home yet; they panicked briefly. No one remembered, later, how this meeting had been arranged. The door of the flat was open; a corridor led to the sitting-room; here, a neutral pattern of furniture awaited them and Bhaskar and Piyu and their mother seated themselves.

Dr Ghosh sat joyously upon an arm-chair facing them. Without delay, he embarked upon an explanation about how his two children, his daughter, Sandhya, and his son, Bipul (the younger of the two, studying management in South India), had grown up looked after by him, because his wife had died twelve years ago of cancer, as if he was recounting an old instructive parable. Over the last five years, the daughter, he confided, had taken over the household.

'Coughs and colds and diarrhoea I can take care of,' he said, 'but not food.' He taught medicine in a college.

'Where is she?' asked Bhola, smiling.

'She's in the kitchen,' said the doctor, too young at fifty to be bereft of a wife, 'making tea. She'll be here in a minute.'

'And what does she do?' asked someone.

'She's doing an MA in sociology, but she's an interior decorator as well ... *That*, I would say' – he smiled – 'is her first love. Everything in this house was decorated by her...' They looked around them with awe at the prints on the walls, the lampshades, and the decorations: wooden Kashmiri miniatures, a picture of a yak and a Tibetan herdsman done with coloured threads.

'It's very quiet here,' said Bhola, 'in spite of being so near the main road! You're lucky to have a flat here, Mr Ghosh.' This congratulatory observation mildly embellished the air of what was a modest but neat flat with breezes circulating in it.

———

Sandhya came out from the kitchen with a tray full of tea-cups and five plates of sweets; they sat up as if they'd been ordered to, and Dr Ghosh said, 'No, you must have something.' She had a peaceful face; she was dark, and wore glasses. No one could decipher from her serenity that she had already seen in the same capacity a cost accountant, a marine engineer, and a lecturer, and been seen; today she had been informed she was to see a businessman's son. No, she was, admittedly, not particularly beautiful, but youth – she was twenty-four – has its own beauty wherever it resides, like a rare flower in a wilderness even in a city as large as Calcutta, an apparition before its bloom fades. Everyone was made speechless by her and Bhaskar glanced at her quickly. They were filled with wonder for a stranger.

'*You* must have one,' said Dr Ghosh to Piyu. 'What's your name? A very pretty girl...'

'Say something,' said her mother.

All her life, except between the age of one and five, when she had been garrulous, albeit with a limited and repetitive vocabulary, Piyu had found talking difficult before strangers, as if she was hiding the best for another encounter, or person.

'Piyali,' she said at last, after a long time.

'We call her Piyu,' said her mother, as if by imparting this fact she had sealed a special pact between them.

———

'Tea?' asked Sandhya suddenly.

So easily these crucial meetings could lapse unobtrusively into boredom! – but this did not happen now. Once Sandhya had poured tea, they considered the sweets and weighed them figuratively. 'The size of these langchaas...' said Bhaskar's mother. Bhaskar said nothing. 'They're fresh,' said Dr Ghosh, as if he were speaking of children he had delivered. 'They come to the sweetshop every evening – I went and bought them an hour ago.' As they ate, he, without undue emphasis, began to ask after Bhola's company. 'We manufacture cranes,' said

Bhola, 'and other kinds of engineering implements.' Bhaskar opened his mouth once or twice, cleared his throat – and said nothing. He put a roshogolla whole in his mouth.

'I saw you devour those sweets,' said his mother, 'you can never resist them'; but that night, when he ate very little at the dining-table, there was palpably some other reason for his loss of appetite.

'What did you think of her?'

His mother put this question to him a few days later, deliberately absent-minded, as if she were questioning the air. A mongrel's bark followed the silence.

She had this evasive way of putting things. Bhaskar knew the question did not need to be answered; that it was a way of postponing what was to and must happen.

'Um,' he said.

Sometimes, when she and Piyu stood together, they, though unconscious of the fact, almost looked as if they came from different families. Piyu was fair; her eyes and forehead were larger than her mother's; but her mother's nose was thinner, sharper, like something she had kept to herself – Piyu's ended in a sort of pleasant, slightly extroverted roundness; light and shade, the future and past, a family's destiny and its inescapable inevitabilities and individualities played around their features, as fate often lights up the moment of a photograph. Manik's face was dominated by his father's, not so much by his features as by the vestiges of his personality. Only with Bhaskar, of whom she was now asking this question, was there a noticeable, fragile similarity of appearance.

———

Winter was about to end now. The trees were in leaf. The winter had made it seem possible that loud choruses and a few clenched fists raised together in the air would delay, perhaps even permanently remove, the prospect of liberalization; would punish the fundamentalists. But as time passed, distractions arose; as February approached March members of the band of players began to drift apart; one person had passed his medical entrance examination; another had got a job; the more serious of the members got more involved in professional theatre and joined professional theatre troupes; the small band broke up.

Now, instructions were issued at the local unit of the Party that cadres must get down to other business: assessing the needs of the locality; assessing its problems; preparing slowly for the next local elections. Whenever Bhaskar thought he would go for a rehearsal he was pressed by some senior cadre to attend a more pressing matter at hand. The streets that used to see the erratic and unexpected outbreak of street-plays were temporarily quieter and bereft of their message, at least as far as one group was concerned. There was also a contradictory rumour in circulation these days that the 'higher-ups' in the Party had, in secret conferences, been forced to reconsider their attitude to liberalization and that at the source of this change was the highest authority himself; reluctantly they began thinking about China on the one hand and Russia on the other.

And the large damp white quilt that had been taken out from a cupboard in the second storey in Vidyasagar Road every November was now, as it grew warmer, folded and laid to rest on the shelf it stayed on in darkness for the rest of the year.

W HEN MINI returned home in the afternoon she found Shantidi in bed in a somewhat odd position, while Anjali the maidservant was sitting and fanning her, shaking her head. As she had come to the staircase she had encountered the familiar damp silence, almost a presence, unkindled by sunlight, but as she had climbed she had sensed subtle signs of disorder she could not quite identify.

'She fell down the stairs, mashima,' she said. 'I had to help her upstairs.'

'But how did you fall?' asked Mini.

Shantidi had slipped two months ago when getting down from a rickshaw in a lane near Chitpur Road but hadn't seriously hurt herself.

'There was something on the stairs,' muttered Shantidi. 'I think it was water . . .' Later, she fell asleep.

I knew this would happen, thought Mini.

Mini thought of the dark stairs and of Shantidi always hurrying, hurrying, towards an unspecified destination.

Next day the pain remained; she woke up with it, found it difficult to move. The pain, just above the thigh and below the hip, distracted Shantidi, but the drama of the situation appeared to amuse her. The drama almost anaesthetized the pain. But soon she grew impatient with her circumscribed condition and struggled briefly with herself, with undescribable movements, because she wanted to resume the daily routine with which she occupied herself, but whose nature very little was really known about. Mini propped her up on the bed and gave her a cup of tea and a Marie biscuit which she dipped cautiously in the tea for it to become soft and red.

It was the flat really, or perhaps just her nature: she could not stand being in one place for too long.

Later, Dr Chakrabarty came and said it could quite possibly be a fracture and that an X-ray would have to be taken.

'Will I have to go to hospital?' said Shantidi. She was like a child about to be shown a new place.

'I think so,' said Dr Chakrabarty. 'Is there no one to help?'

Two sweepers were hired, to their reluctance, from the building (but made more eager by a promise of twenty rupees), to put Shantidi into a chair and then carry her downstairs into a taxi. The two men in khaki shorts proceeded delicately, their knees trembling with the strain, while Shantidi gripped the chair with both hands; and Mini waited to take out twenty rupees from her purse.

That month was spent in journeys to an X-ray clinic, a small hospital with a garden not far away, and in bed rest in the house. Shantidi had taken the chaos almost jubilantly; then, as naturally and inevitably as a seasonal moon passing into a different phase, but unnoticed, she slipped into a deep depression. Mini did not sense it; all her life, Shantidi had been excitable, easily irritable, but intrinsically detached from the frustrations of existence.

She'd retired fifteen years ago for, it appeared to Mini, no good reason. While Mini went to school, Shantidi travelled around most of Calcutta and did not restrict herself to the North. She would turn up at the most unexpected time of the day at people's houses. She'd sat in buses and looked at the workers on Central Avenue and Chowringhee; she'd dozed in traffic jams. Sometimes it was because she had an impulse to see someone; sometimes some child had passed an exam. This was what her early seventies had been like, a simple time of unimpeded, almost incorporeal, mobility.

One day, she said to Mini:

'You're going through a lot of trouble because of my accident.'

'What do you mean?' said Mini, keeping her exercise books on the table. '*I'm* going through a lot of trouble!'

Then, another day, she said:

'Who's going to look after us, Mini?'

Mini sighed. 'Who's looked after us so far?' she said. 'If you look at the way some other people . . .'

'But things don't always stay . . .'

'What is it you're trying to say?' said Mini. 'If we have problems,' she said very practically, 'we'll have to see about them when they come.'

She stayed in school till the afternoon.

'It must be very hot outside,' said Shantidi, ten minutes after Mini had come back. For the door to the small balcony had been shut to protect the room from the heat.

'It *is* hot,' agreed Mini.

'You must be working very hard, Mini,' said Shantidi. 'Especially after I fell.'

153

'What nonsense!'

Sometimes Mini would come back from standing in a queue at the bank, or from the market, and find Shantidi staring, as if she had quite forgotten the numberless tiny routines that made up each day and each week, and as if the world had ceased to exist outside the parameters of her home. Mini counted silently the years since her elder sister had retired, and then how many years it had been since she'd had that liver problem – three – but could come up with no solution. A few days later Shantidi observed, 'I've become a burden on you, Mini.' 'In what way?' Shantidi looked at Mini reproachfully, as if she'd been deceived. 'Because I do nothing. And now I've been laid up in bed,' she said. 'You have to work for both of us, and you're not even well. It would be easier for you, I think, without me,' she said.

Within the flat the heat was bearable. Sometimes a breeze entered the room, but intermittently, because of the block of flats opposite; that building was an obstruction. Yet the walls were cool; it was a flat that became damp during the monsoons.

T HE BOMBS exploded in Bombay.

    The day after the explosions no one wanted to go out but found themselves at work anyway, the usual noises surrounding them.

Mini phoned Khuku.

'*Mini?*' said Khuku. 'You've come to school?'

'What was I to do? I felt I had nothing to do at home.' She began to laugh, then.

'Nothing to do at home!' said Khuku. 'Here was a chance for you to take a day off.'

She herself was planning to leave shortly for the market with two hundred rupees in her purse. There was a pleasurable and wholly fictitious feeling of doom around this simple expedition; it touched everything about her life at the moment.

'Let's see what they do!' she said. 'They won't be able to harm me,' as if she were speaking of a gang of half-wit miscreants to whom it would soon be proved that she was unassailable.

She said then, conspiratorially:

'Suleiman came yesterday . . . He looked quite pleased.'

This mood lasted all day.

THERE, NEAR Mini's house, near the sweet shop with its heavy smell and the decrepit landlords' houses, birds rose almost peacefully into the air.

Thus they would rise habitually from this most ancient part of Calcutta, shriek, and then return a few moments later to balconies and cornices.

In the South, a rather mournful-looking red flag went up by an excavated ditch in the middle of the road. There was no breeze these days, except the slightest one, which caused the flag to flutter.

Towards the end of March, Bhaskar went to see a girl who lived in Jodhpur Park. This meeting was reported to Khuku by Puti, her niece.

'She sings, mashi,' came Puti's voice on the ear-piece. 'So of course Bhola mama asked her to sing. Then he sang a couple of songs himself.'

'Really?'

'Yes.' Puti's laughter filled the space of the ear-piece momentarily. 'But you know Bhola mama, mashi.'

Apparently they had liked the family – it was strange how all the families had been likeable; this particular father occupied a respectable position in a fairly well-known company; and the daughter, 'although no beauty', had 'personality'.

'Is she not good-looking?' asked Khuku.

'Mm.' She thought for an instant. 'They said she has sharp features – a little too sharp, said Abha mami. She's neither dark nor fair.'

'What does Bhaskar think?'

'Bhaskar wants to marry her,' said Puti. 'He liked her very much.'

'But I thought he was going marry the other girl – the one whose mother died of cancer?'

Puti lowered her voice thoughtfully.

'I think Bhaskar likes whoever he meets,' she said. 'Now the first girl is too quiet for him. This one is more talkative.'

———————

Three days after the meeting, the father rang up Bhola: 'Mr Biswas, she's our only daughter; our only child I mean. And to tell you the truth, it's my wife who's a little unsure...' The wife, who'd been so welcoming, so enthusiastic! And was the telephone the right place to vent these misgivings? 'No, I can see why, Mr Lahiri,' said Bhola. He had half expected it. 'But,' said Mr Lahiri, 'if it's not a serious thing – his commitments I mean – because we liked the boy very much...' But Bhola could give the gentleman no such assurance. 'Mr Lahiri,' he said, suddenly moved, 'my son is concerned about things affecting each one of us today ... But I can say that his political ideals don't affect his work or his family life.' 'I quite understand,' said Mr Lahiri.

A DECISION *just* had to be made; would Bhaskar marry, or would he wait? He'd come to set his heart in secret on the last girl, but that now seemed out of the question and the desire almost faded. He had waited; he had waited for a reply that did not come. Then he thought impulsively, 'I must not prolong indefinitely what is after all a wearisome business.' Yet he couldn't bring himself to utter the final syllable. The second girl was what remained; he couldn't recall her face for the moment; but did that matter? 'Say yes,' he said in his own darkness, addressing himself, 'we cannot control our own fate.'

After a few days, Bhaskar agreed to marry the second girl he'd met.

So it was that the match was decided with hardly any of the other relatives knowing about it; they went, ignorant and happy, about their own ways; and even Puti who had a way of hearing about things long before others did remained ignorant. The others who would have heard were kept from this news for about a week; of this union between Vidyasagar Road and a lane off Lansdowne Road.

The girl was two years younger than her son; she's dark, but so am I, thought Bhaskar's mother.

And it'll do him good, she thought, to have some responsibility on his shoulders at last; for I think he still depends too much on his father. His father's growing old; it had hardly occurred to them, because time seems not to affect the people one is closest to; they have a living but transcendental existence in those who love them. He needs to grow up; he's still such a boy; and she thought of him tenderly, in her mind's eye, with a *Ganashakti* in one hand. They all had dreams, but Bhaskar's mother's was practical rather than grandiose; for she hoped, no, she believed, rather calculatingly, that the marriage would divide Bhaskar's energies and weaken his attachment to politics; while Bhaskar's dreams, they were another matter, they were the nation's dreams, or so he believed . . .

There was a plan in her mind, quite cunning, and probably all the more effective because she wasn't entirely conscious of it. She had expected, in truth, it would be a year, even more, before Bhaskar found a girl. But it had happened uncommonly quickly, as if fate itself had decided it should be so and that the problem should be dispensed with. She herself – Bhaskar's mother – remembered when she'd seen her husband's photograph for the first time when she was eighteen and hadn't liked him particularly because he was balding.

———

And thus it happened that the date for the marriage was fixed after Bhola said yes to Dr Ghosh. The parents acted with undue haste, wanting to get it over with as soon as possible, before the two concerned had had a chance to

change their minds. And the summer had only just
to get unpleasantly hot.

The venue for the reception had now to be fixed; th
gravely consulted the calendar with Goodforce Litero
printed on it; and they decided it would be convenient to
have it in a house located five minutes away, across the
main road and the tramlines, which had been renting out
its ground floor for weddings ever since they could
remember. Of course it was a house like any other, but
noticeably at certain times of the year it was transformed
and almost made unrecognizable by lights. Then, later, it
returned to being just another house, but never completely lost its aura of being a house where weddings
were held. Even dates in the summer for this house were
in demand, for people were always getting married whenever there was an auspicious day in the almanac; thus the
17th was already booked, so was the 21st, and so was the
3rd, leaving only the 12th.

THEY BEGAN writing names on envelopes, names of
people who lived in other parts of Calcutta, and in
Pennsylvania and California and England, people who
wouldn't be able to come to the wedding, and might have
even forgotten what Bhaskar looked like; all their names
were written in the heat, and the cards put inside the
envelopes.

'You haven't called Minidi and Shantidi yet,' said Bhaskar's mother.

Bhola looked up.

'I will of course,' he said, and admitted to himself that
he'd forgotten. How could one possibly remember everyone? And this was a time that memory played tricks with
you.

Since moving to Calcutta, they had seen each other
every year except this one. For Mini and Shantidi used
to come religiously by bus once or twice a year to Bhola's
house with a pot of sweets from the north in their hands,
their exultation far exceeding the occasion; and this was
before the roads became bad and when they themselves
were untroubled physically; before their brother had

moved and they became overwhelmed by the weight and pressure of their sheer everyday existence. On those visits, they had seen Bhola struggle with his business; seen Bhaskar growing up and Piyu cram for her exams; seen Bhola's mother as an old and absent woman, and then heard of her death; seen Manik go abroad; been present, in other words, in the semi-lit, casual backstage and dress rehearsals, the unconscious, helpless putting on and putting off of different selves and incarnations, of their lives.

It was afternoon. And in a small lane, in front of a pavement, with the movement of a wrist, something like a curve began to appear, it was not clear what pattern was forming, then the letter D appeared upon the wall of a two-storey house, in black paint, and then U, and N, until DUNKEL had been formed, in the English language, which seemed to blazon itself for its curious purpose; then it began again, and I and M and F began to appear in another corner. Afternoon; no one saw them; it was too hot; on the main road cars went past, up and down; a few people rested; they had eaten; beggars dozed, blind to the heat and shadows, their heads bent to their stomachs. Others on the pavement on the main road, who lived near shop windows or facing tramlines, were still finishing their meals on their plates. Now a picture was forming that would multiply, like an ornate decoration, in different parts of the city, a decoration mirrored, yet seen by almost no one, glanced at perhaps as other thoughts occupied one's head, background to people waiting for buses; yet it told a story. Gatt had been ratified of course; the whole matter had been done with and it had left a wound; yet they went on with these slogans as if they knew something might still come of it. Gradually, on the perfectly good whitewashed wall, there appeared a tiger with the finance minister's turbaned head, a man in coat-tails, a hat that had stars and stripes drawn on it, with a hoop in one hand. The minister, who was, after all, three-quarters tiger, seemed to be polite and full of pleasant intentions but compromised by some invisible fact; he hesitated a moment before he leapt. All else, the figures in the background, the man in the coat-tails, waited; the music had stopped. Only a crow, unseeing, inadvertent, unmindful of human beings, hopped on the pavement again and again, as the spectacle, frozen, unfolded; it appeared to be both searching for, and avoiding, some-thing. Silence echoed all around; even the crow neglected to caw; what would the next action be? Again and again the human-headed tiger seemed to be about to jump but did not. Nikhil, standing and watching, wanted a cup of tea.

WHEN MINI woke up, she reached out for her spectacles. For without them she suffered a temporary darkening of vision.

And then she saw her sister. There was Shantidi, already awake, wandering about on the balcony.

Although Shantidi was better now, and her mild fracture had healed, she had changed to a new, intractable sort of introspection and stubbornness. She would not leave the house.

'What's the matter,' asked Mini finally, 'isn't it tiresome for you to stay here all day? Why don't you start going out a little?'

Shantidi laughed. She shook her head.

'There are things you don't know,' she said. 'There's a reason I don't go out.'

'And what is the reason?' asked Mini.

'You are too trusting, Mini. There are people with their eye on the flat.'

'On *our* flat?' asked Mini, incredulous but nevertheless agitated, her heart beating, with a logic of its own, a little faster. (For over the last two months she'd understood that they could just barely make do on about three thousand rupees a month, but fell short if there were emergencies or accidents. And for the first time the idea came to her of them living in an old age home and that it might be the best future they'd have.)

Shantidi shook her head solemnly. Outside, there was the high-pitched call of a bird that seemed unused to these surroundings.

'Not only our flat – any flat! If the corporation thinks any flat has been left empty, they will take it over and sell it. And there are people over here in the building who are ready to buy another flat to add to their own property. You know that families keep growing,' she gestured around her. 'Besides, there are people living here who have connections with the corporation – what if they go and tell someone?' She spoke with great, knowledge-able practicality, as she always had.

For many years they'd had no one but each other, and sometimes when they spoke they just became two voices, speaking to each other for the sake of speaking, and when they were silent their surroundings became audible.

And Mini wondered where she'd got all her infor-mation – she who had almost broken her leg and had not stirred out of her home for more than a month. She's beginning to have delusions now, sitting here with almost nothing to do, she thought; this is a new development, she concluded interestedly.

'Who told you?' she asked.

'I've heard—' Then, as if to redeem this generality and strengthen her case, she said, 'Mrs Roy told me as well.' And suddenly she looked alone.

There was something in Mini's presence, even as she stood there, small and silent, that imparted peace. It emanated and touched those who were around her.

'But you can go out for a few hours. No one will take possession of the flat if you're away for a short while.'

'Oh no no! You can't say!' said Shantidi. 'These corporation people are capable of anything! And they keep track! They might knock on the door when both of us are away, and say, "Write it down, this flat is empty."'

THERE WAS a by-lane off Central Avenue, on the corner of which there was a shop that dealt in osteopathic aids and implements, part of it facing the main road. Some of these implements were curved and bent fluently, so that they looked like limbs themselves, on the verge of moving, except that they were sturdy and shone, metallic. It was strange the way you might not have seen the shop for years and then one fine day you noticed it. But when someone at school mentioned it to Mini she already knew the place. She thought she might look in and consider buying a special stick of some sort. For actually the pain, which had disappeared almost, was gradually coming back.

A ND NOW Bhaskar wore his white bridegroom's topor;
and Bhola first wore his own dhuti and then tied one
around his son. But Bhaskar's heart fluttered in secret as
if he was nervous before a performance even as outwardly
he managed to appear uniformly either bored or harried;
and he had the merest premonition of coming happiness,
so natural a state that he would already be unable to
remember any other that had preceded it.

All that month Piyu, at her study table, had read for
her tests beneath the light of the table lamp.

The frightening and exhilarated sound of ululation rose
over the other sounds in Vidyasagar Road; it disturbed
some of the children rapt in their textbooks in the other
houses. A wedding was not unusual in the evening though
it might be unexpected at that time of year. And it
reminded one of other things which the city usually kept
secret. People on balconies watched as a car came to pick
up Bhaskar; darkness had settled on almost everything; a
small group of relatives formed temporarily outside the
gates of the house, deterring passers-by. They were
patiently waiting for Bhaskar; he'd gone to the toilet; they
noted that it was twenty-five minutes to the auspicious
moment, the lagna, and hoped he wouldn't be long ... but

here he was! Then they got into the car; Bhola, his heart in his mouth, and other relatives would follow in their cars through Vidyasagar Road and Ashutosh Mukherjee Road.

It was a little after sunset that it had begun; now it was, to all purposes, night, but a stream of commerce and transactions between human beings continued in aggregations of localities, oblivious to everything else. Some people had come all the way from Shyambazar and Paikpara, with children who had their heads stuck out of the car window most of the way and had to have their hair combed before they got out. Later, there would be people eating at the tables whom no one recognized.

The slow but by now palpable approach of Bhaskar's car set into motion a small, winglike flutter of panic among the waiting children, cries of 'Here's the bridegroom!', and much tripping on the folds of the unfamiliar garments they were enveloped in. Once more that unearthly ulula- tion was heard, like nothing issuing from the voices of humans. In Sandhya's father's heart, as he walked forth swiftly, there was a stirring, like a stab of pain, for his motherless daughter. And in Vidyasagar Road, Bhaskar's mother, who would arrive later, sat alone with herself as company, become a shadow in the house she'd come to so many years ago.

And when Bhaskar saw the priests, he was startled and mystified. For he had forgotten the sacredness of the enterprise, the pact with ancestry, caste, and divinity which the two priests would make on his behalf. And they would evidently be his wayfarers and guides for the next hour or so.

Both of the priests were touchingly and shabbily self-conscious on the occasion, as a recently married couple might be caught waking up at home. One of them had hair that was oiled and combed back; and the other one, when he opened his mouth, revealed he had a couple of teeth missing.

'I'll take the Gold Spot!'

'Would you like a Gold Spot, Uncle?'

'Bring one here!'

The children were fighting to serve soft drinks.

'It's not quite a bourgeois affair, is it?'

'I suppose not. What can you say about weddings though – our mothers and fathers did it the same way.'

'Our parents did a lot of things that ... ask that boy for a Gold Spot.'

Two Party members, in somewhat loud clothes, unusually happy, talking above the music, were inhaling the perfume of sandalwood in smoke and exploring the territory.

He had to look at Sandhya and she at him; the division – a white cloth – was removed. His relatives were teasing him and he had begun to be irritable; he remembered that one meeting they had had, and that he had not dared to look at her properly then, and this seemed to him almost a continuation of that very meeting. 'Ei, look at him,' cried her cousins; and she did finally, and smiled, as if at a private thought.

After an hour they both got up at the priest's command

to walk seven times around the fire. When he sat down again, he thought he would open a conversation and say, 'It's hot, isn't it?' but did not. When Mohit and Sameer and his cousin Arnab approached him to speak to him, as if he had been smuggled into another world but could still communicate in monosyllables with this one, he answered over the droning of the priests with a casual smile and murmur. His nostrils were full of smoke and, now and then, the smell of sandalwood. She seemed quite stoic and self-assured, wiping away the perspiration from her forehead. It was a moment of great loneliness for them, as they sat there, not understanding the mantras; what seemed to be boredom in them was actually an odd, vacant melancholy; but, meanwhile, the photographers craned over each other, bumping into relatives, while the flash-bulbs went off.

They had been asked to repeat their own names; their parents' names; each other's names; they had been wished well, in a Sanskrit they did not understand, and a happy married life by Tradition, in the person of these priests. Then one of the priests said, 'It's finished,' to Bhaskar as he rose, surreptitiously, as if imparting a bit of taboo information before leaving. For they had been asked by Bhola to complete the rituals as quickly as they could and had managed to abbreviate a few things and skim guilelessly over others (and dilate a few stanzas, since they were being paid by the hour) and they had finished in just under two hours. The wedding was over, and, though no one appeared to have noticed and they themselves were almost ignorant of it, the two – the young man, who evidently had a backache, and the young woman – were now married. They were at a loss as to what to do now; they had the puzzled air of people who'd just knocked on a door and were on the verge of turning round without having heard a reply from within.

———

But it was difficult to come to terms with how ordinary it was. The new dhuti was already crumpled; and Bhaskar was wearing his kurta again, shyly.

A bed had been made for them, and complex garlands and tassels of flowers, painstakingly created, hung on all sides around it to enclose the two, at some future moment, in privacy. When they would go, eventually, to Vidyasagar Road, this bed would go with them and climb lightly up all the stairs to Bhaskar's room.

———

And after another three days, when Bhaskar had brought his bride to his house and promised, at a ceremony, to provide her with food and clothes for the rest of her life, he grew drowsy; he had spent three days eating.

In the evening, Sandhya took off her wedding sari and went into the bathroom – an interval passed in which her absence was not noticed – and she emerged wearing a red cotton sari, her hair wet. She folded the Benarasi she had been wearing and asked Bhaskar's mother, 'Where should I keep this?'

THEY WERE in the large room on the second floor, where Bhaskar used to sleep alone. That night they sat on the bed, with gifts on every side.

She seemed reticent.

'That light is so bare,' she said, pointing to a light attached to the wall, 'it should have a lamp-shade.'

He looked at the light.

'Were you tired today?' he asked without sincerity.

'No – were you?' she asked, folding handkerchiefs that had been received as a gift.

'Not really,' he said, suppressing a yawn. 'Though I *am* feeling a little sleepy.' They spoke as if they'd known each other for years, while Vidyasagar Road unfolded before them, invisibly, as if it had never changed. He immediately regretted saying this, because he wanted to talk to her; but his eyes were red and tired.

Later, he went and changed into his kurta and pyjamas and returned and lay upon the bed. Sandhya came out of the bathroom wearing a nightie, tying her hair into a plait. Her shadow hovered upon the wall, trying to find its home here.

'Where does Piyu sleep?' she asked thoughtfully.

'Downstairs,' he replied.

She considered this silently. Entire childhoods had

passed in this room, like a light going out, that she could only sense unclearly. He didn't know what to do next. As she sat on the bed, he turned around again; he glanced at her narrow back, at the dark skin above the neck of her nightie, the colour of her shoulders. And he wondered why she had decided to marry him; it was probably some entirely trivial reason, something he should be able to imagine but couldn't. Plausibly, almost touchingly, there might be no good reason: how mysterious the world was at every moment, the birth of love and generations. The nightie, starched cotton, was a pattern of pink flowers with white borders, almost like a curtain, probably made recently by some tailor or chosen from ten nighties that looked nearly the same at some shop; and when she lay down beside him, he scratched his arm and pretended to be tired. But he also felt the guilty, obtrusive stirring of desire; he kept it to himself, instinct or some genetically inherited knowledge instructing him that there was a decorum about these things he must observe. They still had a few of the ornamental marks that had been made along their faces and foreheads, which hadn't come off with soap; Sandhya's having been made by an aunt, widowed, forty-two years old, watched by her two twelve-year-old daughters (they were twins). But Sandhya had never known before now, the eve of her wedding, the minor artistic accomplishments this aunt, who lived on Vivekananda Road, possessed; actually, she did not know her very well; but she had, with a clove dipped repeatedly in sandalwood paste, made, with every tiny pin-prick impress, those subtle marks on her forehead. If there was one thing she would have liked to keep from that day it would have been these patterns.

'I have to wake up early tomorrow,' he muttered, waiting

to see what she would say. But she didn't protest; she had wavy hair; he saw that she had dark lips; the calm sound of the fan repeatedly filled the silence. 'Are you missing home?' he said, turning on his side and letting his hand fall near her shoulder; he had acquired a small belly, and she seemed thin in comparison to him. This morning, she had cried when leaving her house. 'No, not really,' she said, quite gravely, like a child who has had a new experience. It was strange; they'd spoken with each other at length two nights ago in the rented room in that house in which they'd been married; and they had forgotten, for the time being, what they had talked about and would almost have to be reacquainted with each other. Bhaskar switched off the light and they tried to fall asleep. He had not known before how shy he was with the opposite sex. It was an uncomfortable night; whenever a car passed through the lane, its headlights lit up the wall of the room, and towards dawn, a kitten mewed and sounded like a child crying. Each sound set the tympanum in the inner ear vibrating.

Towards dawn he awoke and gazed unsurprised at her as she slept, her eyelids momentarily parted to reveal the blue-grey light in her eyeball. But she was not awake, and everywhere there were only the merest signs of life; the blue dawn; a reticent vibration from the tramline; the early insistent cry of a shalik; her breath; in each of these life resided on the edge of itself. Meanwhile the fan lulled them.

When Bhaskar woke up again, he found she was not there. He was surrounded by the sound of crows and buses and rickshaws and the tube-well and schoolchildren, all things apparently in perpetual transit. Going down, he was startled to see that she had joined his parents and Piyu for breakfast in the room where they all ate.

'WHERE SHOULD I put these?'
      Sandhya was holding a chain from which a golden locket hung. She held it, weightless, in her palm.

'Let's put this one back in its box,' said Bhaskar's mother. They bent forward like two conspirators. Light glinted and scattered.

It was one of the things she had given her. Last month she had taken a bus and gone to the jeweller's and had had a necklace and a pair of earrings 'broken' and converted into this longer, this more beautiful piece. And she felt a strange tenderness towards it that was not unconnected to loss, for what was once hers had become something else and someone else's.

Her youth lived on in the forms these jewels took. And whenever Bhaskar's mother felt that familiar boredom coming on with a piece of jewellery, she would take the piece, like a child with a toy, to the jeweller who had first made it and describe in words the new design, and leave the piece with him as if she were lending it to him; and he would give it back to her made 'new' in five days. Sometimes, when the piece was not very old, one suffered a small loss, for the jeweller subtracted about a tenth of the gold as part of his fee.

When she was young gold had been cheap, and she

remembered those beloved thick bangles and that floral necklace she'd got when she was married.

After Bhola had left his job and embarked upon his business, Bhaskar's mother had been protective and uncompromising about one thing: her jewellery. She was wise; for it was instinct rather than experience that told her that once he started using her gold to cover his business losses, it would happen again and again. But it had to be admitted that he had never made such a request. And this disinterested emblem of beauty and desire, the soul's continual yearning for celebration, so removed from the everyday, which would one day belong entirely to her children, to Piyu or to her sons' wives, remained untouched.

———

Two days later they stripped the bed of its floral covering; some of the flowers had dried and fallen to the floor, from where they were swept away by Haridasi. For Haridasi, Bhaskar's wedding and the bride's arrival had been events touched with wonder. It had certainly been the biggest change in the household since she'd come to work here. She had looked carefully at the bride, and thought she was graceful, if not beautiful. And the bride too had glanced at her once or twice.

———

Bhaskar's father-in-law began to visit late in the morning.

'Come in, come in,' Bhaskar's mother would say from the veranda when he rang the bell. She would feel strangely embarrassed, as if she wanted to keep something hidden from him. During the wedding, under the artificial canopy, the world shut out, she'd had trouble recognizing him; there they were, like two actors from separate plays, having met in a strange place, hot now at the end of it, he poised, she uncomfortable and glowing with the heat. Twice since the wedding she had seen him in dreams, in the first one arriving at their house bearing gifts and in the second inexplicably displeased about something. Ever since then her vision of him had been oddly prejudiced, as if she, to her discomfort, knew something about him that no one else did.

Sandhya would race down the stairs barefoot from the second storey.

'It's terrible out there,' he would say, coming up.

Bhaskar's mother did not quite know how to take him. And she was wearing a green sari which she wore when doing housework.

He didn't seem to notice.

'It is easy to see,' he would say, 'that this is a house which a lady takes pleasure in keeping tidy.'

From his second visit onward he would go straight up to the second storey; there he would sit talking with his daughter for an hour. On his way out he would shout a farewell to Bhaskar's mother.

He would come at all times of the day, but mainly in the morning.

What do they talk about? she would think.

'ARE THOSE your parents, ma?' asked Sandhya.

There were two pictures on the wall on this side of the room, one of Bhaskar's mother's father, another of her mother. Like them, she too, the new bride, did not feel that she as yet fully existed in this house. They considered this world from the hereafter with a certain immediacy; they both had daubs of vermilion on their foreheads that looked like they still hadn't quite dried. Outside, a summer that distributed, unequally, shadows and heat had settled down on Vidyasagar Road.

'Yes,' said Bhaskar's mother. 'And those are baba's mother and father.'

A smell of cooking drifted up stealthily from downstairs. And she, the newly married one, turned her eyes towards a large framed black and white photograph of an old woman in a white sari, sitting on what looked like a chair, and another of Bhola's father wearing a moustache. The tops of the frames had become brown with a kind of fine powder as if they hadn't been dusted for weeks. These photographs had been hanging there for almost twenty years now; and now their eyes gazed upon this couple each morning. She – the grandmother – had come to Bhola's father as his second wife, after the death of his first one, sixteen years old at the time of marriage and only thirty-two when her husband died. Only her children remembered now that she had had a gift for mathematics and had won a gold medal at school, but had forfeited her studies after marriage, much to the disappointment of her schoolteacher, an Englishwoman, a disappointment that the sixteen-year-old herself couldn't understand. Along the wall, all the parents were joined together in eternal life, and a peripatetic gecko was known to live behind these portraits, curved, alone, arbitrarily moving from one frame to another. And Bhola's father was a mystery; no one in this house had set eyes upon him because he had died a few months before Bhola's birth. In that death lay the key to this family's early misery, and their subsequent search for order and balance.

And now they said he had been a King's Commission Engineer, one of the 'heaven-born'. But, after he died, the family had been left with nothing; and later he had become this portrait in this house on Vidyasagar Road gifted to Bhola by his father-in-law, now confronted by Sandhya. Something of his aptitude and perhaps the romance of engineering had been inherited by the family, shaping and influencing lives that were generations removed from him; generations to come that had never known him; for Borda's younger son was an engineer; Bhola had tried to cast himself in his father's mould and become a civil engineer, and created Goodforce Literod Ltd.; even Manik was studying engineering in Germany. In this way the grandfather that no one knew had lived on in his children's and grandchildren's lives.

———

Summer was everywhere. Meanwhile, Sandhya began to embroider a piece of cloth and make a doll's dress inside her room. She was always making things; now a bangled hand pushed a thread through a needle. One shoulder leaning on an elbow, her sari's aanchal falling abstractedly from her back, she pursued her handiwork.

Bhaskar was still something of an enigma in her life; she hardly knew him at all; and he reappeared in the evenings after his long journey from Howrah, tired. Then he would wash his face and feet beneath the tap in the small bathroom and there would be a far-away rush of running water. Emerging, he would quickly survey his reflection hovering darkly in the bedside mirror. One evening, lying on the bed in the glare of the electric light, he asked her:

'What's this?'

For he had picked up the small shiny blue dress that had been left inadvertently next to a pillow. It was as if some tiny, subtle spirit that had perhaps visited this room had divested herself of her clothing before disappearing.

'Oh, that ... that's something I made over the last two days when I had nothing else to do,' she said, raising her face briefly.

He lifted it nakedly up to the light.

'It's a little small for you,' he said, indifferent.

S HE KNEW very little about the company, too little; nothing but seeing Bhaskar become each morning a person who wore pleated trousers and a shirt and shoes before disappearing to a factory that made cranes. 'Take me to it one day,' she said without meaning it.

And he knew nothing about her. In marrying each other they had in effect embraced the unknown and the inconsequential. To look at, she might have been anyone; sometimes he would notice how her shoulders looked tenderly hunched and rounded when she was sitting down; the next day he checked to see if it was still true, as if reality could not be relied upon not to change at short intervals; during this time everything he saw in her he saw with a child's guilty and inquisitive eye.

But she and her husband hardly had any time together. They met in the morning at the dining-table as acquaintances would, the reverberations of night-time already having faded and left them almost more distant from each other. Bhaskar did not look at her in the presence of others; he as good as pretended she wasn't there; and then he was gone for most of the day. The first days of their marriage was a time of trust in the unproven and of unspoken longing.

Having grown up elsewhere, she had no friends in

Calcutta. A few relatives lived on the outskirts of Calcutta, and others even further away. Now and then her brother appeared, dark and bespectacled and much like her to look at, and then disappeared again. And for the first month and a half of their marriage, Bhaskar took her quite for granted.

At night their fingers and hands crept towards each other, in the greed for closeness, and for those sensations, only incompletely experienced so far, of something between pain and satisfaction, concealment, and happiness.

Upstairs was where their new life began, beneath the photographs of late and everpresent grandparents. Where Bhaskar's and Manik's and Piyu's childhood had begun and evolved and come to a conclusion, where they'd slept together on the bed in often anarchic and filial positions, played between and under the beds and bruised themselves, another existence began at last.

———

She had become used to the lane which, at first, had kept her from sleep.

Early in the morning, when it was not quite light, she sometimes sensed him going out; it was inexplicable; she sighed; and then once or twice she saw him return with a pile of newspapers, the *Ganashakti*. It was a paper she'd never read; but Bhaskar insisted to her, with what seemed to her an excessive and uncomfortable advocacy, that it contained all the real and important news and all that was really worth reading. She didn't believe him; for *Ganashakti* was a paper that no one she knew read; it was, as far as she knew, used to make cartons and containers in the market; and its pages were swept away in lanes and alleys. These early morning excursions of his became indistinguishable to her sometimes from the intense dreams she had before waking.

She kept herself to herself and still hadn't quite made friends with the family. During her solitary explorations, she found old comic books, toys, beneath the staircase to the terrace. And she discovered near a doll with an arm missing and a Ludo board a set of tiny pots and pans – kitchen utensils. Though they were old now, they must have once been used by Piyu to cook make-believe meals for an imaginary husband and family, or probably just for the sake of imitating the motions of cooking. How possessive children are about their imaginary homes! – almost as proprietorial as they are when they grow up and have real ones. Sandhya found them when clearing away piles of other things that had been dumped beneath the stairs to the terrace (she was beginning to rearrange this floor which would be her household), their small but exact shapes lying overturned, but still intact.

And then she put artificial flowers and leaves, imitations of tulips, roses, in two vases. She had loved these so much, almost as if they were alive – she had bought them from a small stall in Gariahat and carried them back crowded in her arms. They, however, turned out to be a less than perfect replica, the edge of the leaf frayed, with a few short strands of loose thread hanging from it.

'Why don't you get real flowers?' asked Bhaskar one day.

'If I have real flowers,' said Sandhya, 'they'll die in a

couple of days – and then who'll give me the money to buy new ones: you?'

'But these will get dirty in a week,' he said.

'They won't,' said Sandhya, aware of some protective magic which would keep the dust from getting to the flowers; and with such conviction did she say it that for a moment Bhaskar was convinced as well. Thus the perennially blooming flowers, cheap, bright, immortal blossoms, remained.

THEY HAD still not been on their 'honeymoon'; and the crows made an unbroken, troubled din outside and hopped about relentlessly. But they'd put all the cheques they'd got as wedding presents into a bank account; part of it they'd use for their trip. And as they spoke, weighing the size of their budget against their expected expenditure, India, in their imaginations, became a series of small hotels, connecting routes, different climates existing at once, peculiarities of cuisine.

She'd always wanted to go to Kashmir. And yet that paradise had been poisoned. How wonderful it was to wander through India with your parents as a child (she blurredly remembered travelling to strange places – this was such a large country – when her mother was alive; there was no death then, nor destiny), then to forget most of it, except a stomach upset that had made you sick or a sari being bought by your mother in a shop or the paleness of a white hotel façade, and then have a sense of it come back to you many years later as you prepared to make the journey with another person, almost a stranger.

For a few days, they – Bhaskar's relatives – had been waiting to see if Bhaskar, upon getting married, would gradually relinquish his commitment to the Party and take up a more respectable form of existence. The Party was spoken of as an illicit but persistent liaison.

'But I don't think Sandhya will allow him to continue for long.'

Someone else said: 'She's a hard-headed sensible girl after all.'

'Let us see.'

They waited. But married life and its responsibilities seemed to leave Bhaskar unchanged. He was still selling *Ganashakti*; and, even now, he would, vociferously if necessary, and for as long as he could, marshalling an array of facts and arguments, criticize the new and sinister global order, the present government that was governing shamelessly from the centre, illegal bargains between nations and business houses, and every relative, cousin, or uncle who happened to disagree with him.

CRPF SOLDIERS; three months ago, and before then, they'd appeared when the roads were silent, waiting for riots to break out in the city though they eventually hadn't. Sleepy-eyed, waving at the children. As if they were passing through, a peacekeeping force on their way elsewhere.

And yesterday, going through Ballygunge and Park Circus, a truckload that not everyone noticed. These sleepy, sometimes smiling men. Although they were so still now, they could be cruel. Waiting patiently in the traffic jam like the others, their job probably long done...

THEY — BHASKAR and the wife he hardly knew — made preparations for the journey, preparations to be absent from the house for five days. From responsibilities and business partners, parents and parents-in-law, the meetings in the evening, they decided to take a train to Siliguri, and from there a bus to Darjeeling. People had taken the route many times before and many had it by heart; it was like a well-known line of poetry.

They passed roads that had been made by the British, connecting Bengal to the rest of the country, and which were still more or less unchanged, passing the dirty ponds and warm villages of Bengal, hungry children and women with their heads lowered, bulls sunning themselves; INDIA IS GREAT said the message that disappeared between two places; Bhaskar saw these things as a husband and a holiday-maker rather than one who'd become involved in the struggle; they were accompanied in the train by a Bengali family, by old women, and children with colds; they had with them two suitcases, a flask, and a tiffin carrier.

Street-theatre, old forlorn papers: rummaging upstairs for something else, Bhaskar's mother discovered, grown damp with moisture, photocopied manuscripts among a heap of discarded desiderata and wondered what they were.

'When he's back,' she said when two days had passed, 'I want him to see the doctor again.'

'Why? Does he still have that backache?' asked Bhola.

'I think so. It's the way he bends at times. He does it slowly and hesitantly, as if it's a luxury.'

A ND KHUKU lay on her bed in the afternoon. Although her eyes were closed, she was wide awake, she could hear Nando quarrelling, and she wondered if it was good for Shib to be in that office in this heat at this age: she didn't like it. Outside, in the blank heat, the sun pulsed like a star that could not be seen.

Oh, men must work; nothing else makes them as happy. But she lay there, cross, unable to sleep.

There was movement in the clouds outside, and lightning; it stirred the air. Shib came back to her as he used to be when he was a boy, when he visited their home so often that she was hardly aware of him, but unaware of him in a different way from her unawareness of him now; a different way of taking someone's presence for granted. How like a ghost that boy was, both in his paleness and in the strangeness his memory had assumed. He was her brother Pulu's best friend, a boy whose quietness was deceptive because he noticed more than he appeared to. He was wavy-haired, as he was now, and used to be unusually fair-skinned, more so then than he was at present. He had no mother; she had died when he was two years old, and he'd never had any memory of her. He used to be shy when he came to their house, and her own mother had a special fondness for him because he was motherless and an only child. Thus there was that lost quality about him, even though he belonged to one of the most well-to-do families in the town.

Unanswerable, obsolete questions glimmered in the flashes of lightning. What would have happened to Khuku if Shib had not married her? After school, Khuku's family had stopped her college education because they said they could not afford it; it was probably true. 'But Khuku was never interested in schoolwork anyway,' her brother said in explanation. She had cried for a week, for herself and in forgiveness. A vacancy opened up before her as one kind of life receded from her permanently, the world of exams and preparations and the panic of examination day, now only to be known in other people's lives. Then she had stayed at home and practised on the harmonium. She had read new novels, and entered into an imaginary world. Characters in stories became as real to her as people; like Khenti who loved pui leaves, and tender-hearted Goshtho didi in *Mahasthabir Jatak*. Years passed. She read; she waited; she waited silently for some change. She knew, instinctively, she wouldn't end in the place she'd begun in. They grew up – brothers, sisters, friends; Khuku, Bhola, Shib, Mini, not knowing where they would live, what their children would look like, who their spouses would be, in what way their lives would be different from each other's, or what incarnation the world would take fifty years from now. At the beginning, they'd moved blindly from birth into the unknown, from darkness into the world; the passage into life, as the one through it, is a journey, and they, unlike the ones who had died in mid-life or as children, had been deemed to complete it, to live out their days in the world.

She hadn't even realized that Shib thought of her in a particular way. (Shib said that it was her singing that had decided him; and this alarmed her; what if she had not been able to sing?) But Khuku's elder sister, that stern woman and tender romantic, would always say later, 'I knew it. When Khuku pinched Shib once, and I saw Shib blush, I knew it.' Khuku herself had had no idea. When he first proposed to her, in a roundabout way, through her mother, she refused without hesitation. 'But I don't think of him in that way!' she said. 'He's more like a brother to me...' Her mother had said, 'Think again. You won't find another like him.' But Khuku hesitated; she was certain she was in love with someone else. How intense and chastening these emotions seemed now! On and on one goes, gradually to become a stranger to oneself, but never completely, and never knowing what it is that pushes us in one direction and not another... And how deeply they believed in romantic love in those days: it was all those long novels. She procrastinated; she neither said no nor yes. Then one day, after she had finished singing a song, she saw a kindness on Shib's face she had not noticed before; it had always been there, but she had not seen it; it was as if she'd suddenly recognized who he was. Soon after they were engaged, and Shib went to England; and, after six years, she followed him there. It was a few years after Independence; Shib's father had died; he knew he would never return home. Their marriage was thus a marriage of childhood acquaintances, of two people who had known each other when they had hardly mattered to one another and who had grown one day into their shared life without hardly being aware of it; only slightly embarrassed when that awareness came. And their new life, under some nameless star, began with each other.

THEN SHE remembered her friend's arthritis, and the pain, persistent, monotonous, as personal as something imagined, which was born of neglect and carelessness. Yet the thing about arthritis was that you didn't know why it happened to one person and not to another; there appeared to be no clearly identifiable cause; it was yet another mystery that governed and left its casual impress upon existence. 'It's four months now,' she thought, and recalled that Mini should have been back in three months for another check-up. And yet the thought of Mini, whose every trouble filled her with a sense of responsibility, also, contradictorily, brought to her a feeling of happiness and excitement.

The last time she'd called her was when there had been an explosion in Central Avenue, not very far from Mini's building; and they'd trembled and thought that the troubles had begun in Calcutta. But no, to their relief, but almost to their disappointment as well (for they succumbed easily to excitement), it was the arsenal of a local hoodlum that had blown up by accident.

'I wonder how she is,' thought Khuku (for Mini came back to her as a person in a dream), and dialled the number of her school. 'Hello?' she said. 'Can I speak to Supriti Biswas?' The person at the other end seemed to weigh this question and consider its merits. Supriti Biswas. In a voice that sounded slightly put out, the person eventually relented and said, 'Hold on a minute, please.'

There was a gap of five minutes. She heard the voices of children, random and happy, in the ear-piece. Then a voice she knew well said, 'Khuku?'

———

Later she grew sleepy; the talk had relaxed her. The light of oncoming dusk played and scattered on the large windows. It scattered and seemed to vanish but remained like a glaze. A thought came to her: I'll go there tomorrow; she said she'd be at home.

She'd fall asleep now as usual in the middle of the afternoon and wake up unable to tell for how long she'd slept, whether it was ten minutes or half an hour or more. Why, sometimes it seemed to her she'd fallen asleep as a child and woken up to find that most of her life had passed by; she was here.

A visit to a friend's house has its own secrecy. Sometimes it seems that there is no reason, except a slight sense of boredom, a hint of life's emptiness, a memory of familiarity and a promise of pleasure. Half asleep already, she prepared herself for the journey.

Five years ago, after her husband had retired, she'd come to this city with some trepidation and uncertainty to make her home here in old age. The young leave this city if they can; the old, it seems, return to it; and this had been the incentive for coming here – the possibility of experiencing, in early old age, the buoyancy of visiting known houses through these roads, of watching the old apparently arrest and embrace time as children and grandchildren grow taller and older, surprising one.

And there were friends, which she hadn't thought of then. Every time she went to the New Municipal Corporation Buildings with its strange E-shaped block of flats off Central Avenue it was as if something had changed slightly from before and she couldn't put her finger on it. The route was familiar, though, the dust and reconstruction and disrepair. It was not so much a return to childhood for her as a contact with something she'd known for a long time, in conditions neither she nor her friend could have foreseen. And now, very lightly, like a merciful gift of remembrance, obliterating as it engendered, it began to rain. It fell on the graffiti on the walls inside lanes, the hammer and sickle that multiplied everywhere and the pleas for family planning, the advertisements for companies; it first rained on South Calcutta and then moved towards the North, the clouds prefiguring, and desultorily washing, the route Khuku would take.

I'll take a flask of tea and some sweets from Mahaprabhu, she thought.

For she didn't want Mini or Shantidi in the kitchen once she'd arrived.

Must tell that rascal straight away, she decided, thinking of Nando. Of course, if I tell him now he'll forget about it tomorrow.

She must remind that shirker to put the tea in the flask the first thing the next morning.